Different Beasts

DIFFERENT BEASTS

J.R. McCONVEY

stories

Excerpt from "Skunk Hour" from *New Selected Poems* by Robert Lowell, edited by
Katie Peterson. Copyright © 2017 by Harriet Lowell and Sheridan Lowell.
Reprinted by permission of Farrar, Straus and Giroux.

Edited by Bethany Gibson.
Cover and page design by Julie Scriver.
Cover images detailed from *Two Beasts I*, copyright © 2019
by Anna Torma, annatorma.com.
Printed in Canada.
10 9 8 7 6 5 4 3 2 1

Library and Archives Canada Cataloguing in Publication

Title: Different beasts : stories / J.R. McConvey.
Names: McConvey, J. R., 1979- author.
Identifiers: Canadiana (ebook) 2019008975X | Canadiana (print) 20190089725 |
ISBN 9781773101279 (EPUB) | ISBN 9781773101286 (Kindle) |
ISBN 9781773101262 (softcover)
Classification: LCC PS8625.C665 D54 2019 | DDC C813/.6—dc23

Goose Lane acknowledges the generous support of the Government of Canada,
the Canada Council for the Arts, and the Government of New Brunswick.

Goose Lane Editions
500 Beaverbrook Court, Suite 330
Fredericton, New Brunswick
CANADA E3B 5X4
www.gooselane.com

MIX
Paper from
responsible sources
FSC® C103567

To my mother, for reading to me;
to Amy, for reading with me;
and to Danica, for teaching me to read again.

I myself am hell;
nobody's here—

only skunks, that search
in the moonlight for a bite to eat

—Robert Lowell, "Skunk Hour"

Contents

Contents

How the Grizzly Came to Hang in the Royal Oak Hotel

One day a bear got loose in the Royal Oak Hotel. This was in the early years of my employment there, shortly after my discharge, when it hardly felt real to be out in the world. They were using the lobby to shoot a scene for an action film that featured a grizzly bear attack. While it could have been done digitally, the director was a Hollywood type who insisted on flying in a wild bear from the Yukon for maximum effect. Local animal rights groups filed a complaint with the city and went to the media, calling it cruelty. On the morning of the shoot, news vans from all the big networks came to film the protest being staged out front of the hotel. A few dozen people showed up to chant slogans and wave signs covered with drawings of crucified teddy bears. But the director went ahead with his plan.

So I guess you could call what happened poetic justice, if you believe justice ever reads like a poem, or that any true poet would take carnage for a muse.

That day, the hotel lobby was packed. There were security guards, conservation officers carrying tranquilizer guns, bear handlers reeking of salmon jerky treats. None of it mattered. Three days prior, the bear had been plucked from an alpine meadow on the slopes of Kluane Lake, away from the woods and the water and the ambient scent of prey, and herded onto a cargo plane for a quick flight across the continent into an urban nightmare. The drastic change in its environment, combined with a bootcamp training schedule, had finally flabbergasted it into attack mode. As soon as the klieg lights were turned on it, the bear went berserk, storming around the lobby, mauling two guards and a production intern with running swats that almost looked tossed off, just for the hell of it, then stampeded the craft services table and knocked out the lights and began doing furious laps of the perimeter, its huge claws skittering across the polished marble floors. In the chaos someone managed to corral it into Banquet Room C, a windowless auditorium just north of the reception desk, and barricade the doors with a sofa, giving everyone time to tend to the injured and work out what to do next.

They might have ended up resolving the situation sensibly if the Congressman hadn't been staying at the hotel. He was visiting from south of the border to gauge support for a new pipeline project, a man known for loud suits and louder opinions. As soon as he heard that the grizzly had run amok, he stormed into the trashed lobby with his sleeves rolled up, grinning and talking at inspirational volume about "the right way to deal with this kind of a situation." It was as though Palm Sunday had come early and here was Christ preaching his way into Jerusalem, vowing to throw the thieves from the temple, the camera crews trailing faithfully behind.

It was evident that the Congressman intended to shoot the bear. A tentative call had been made to try and tranquilize the grizzly, cage it and drive it to a compound outside the city, where the handlers could recondition it. The Congressman, though, sensed a moment he could leverage. Speaking to an array of cameras, he emphasized the ongoing threat. He asked, if a city couldn't properly defend itself against a dumb animal, what chance would it have against terrorists or an invading army? In his opinion, as long as it was alive, the bear presented a significant danger to the public. Waving his arm out over the lobby, he insisted that his number one priority was safety for the people.

There were objections, of course. The conservation officers questioned the Congressman's jurisdiction, protesting that he had no authority outside his own borders. The handlers, who were responsible for the bear and would legally own it after the shoot, threw fits and threatened to sue. An animal rights activist who'd managed to sneak in shouted that he would cut the Congressman's balls off, but security dragged him away. I watched the various parties' faces fall into numb horror as they came to understand that the Congressman would simply ignore their protests and do as he liked. There might be some settlement later, suits filed and money exchanged. But the show had to go on.

It more or less closed the matter when the Congressman pulled the vintage Colt single-action .357 Magnum revolver from the holster under his vest and told the cameras that with the expansion bullets he was using, he could drop the bear at twenty paces, no problem, before any innocent bystanders were maimed or killed. By that point, with the question of the city's weakness at stake, its ability to protect its own citizens, it was impossible to deny him outright. Besides, he had reporters following him, which shored up the impression that his opinion was gospel. Even the director, a maestro of self-importance, deferred to the authority of the cameras.

His clout aside, it was clear that the Congressman couldn't be allowed to just kick down the banquet room doors and open fire. The optics wouldn't work. So the manager of the hotel stepped in, ostensibly to express further outrage, yelling righteously and pointing out that it wasn't even legal for the Congressman to be carrying a handgun up here. But you could tell from the outset that there was more to it. He felt he was being upstaged. As manager, he said, it fell to him to make decisions about the hotel. Furthermore, the Royal Oak promised the highest-quality luxury hotel experience, and he insisted on taking full personal responsibility for the gross inconvenience to his guests.

The two men chirped back and forth for a while, and my attention wandered, as it often did at work. I don't remember how long it took them to decide. But I can remember the exact moment when I saw the manager turn and point at me.

The manager knew my situation and enough of my history that, although there were plenty of more qualified people there, I guess I was the politically expedient choice. I stayed quiet while he laid out what was expected of me. It was nothing unusual; I knew how to follow orders. I thought about my sister, Sara, how she'd pulled every string she had to land me this job. I remembered the look of uncertainty on her face when she told me they were willing to give me a try. Taking advantage of his moment with the cameras, the manager explained how the hotel's reputation was at stake, and how of course they couldn't have an esteemed guest like the Congressman carry the whole burden of this errand on his own. I knew better than to protest when he started talking about heroes and casually dropped a reference to Afghanistan, as though it were a dash of spice, something to sprinkle on his speech for flavour.

It was in what he didn't mention—Kandahar and the tribunal, the detainees kneeling with black sacks pulled over their heads, the famous photograph of me that tells a story I don't remember, my time in the psych wing of the veterans' hospital—that I knew I had no choice in the matter.

I remember thinking how this was just another day to them, the manager and the Congressman and the media, as though the hotel lobby was the scene of such spectacles all the time, and if they just put their heads together and stayed the course, everything would turn out all right. They believed, without question, in their own truth. You could see the fever in their eyes, though, the tremor in their hands—the seething need to take the violence they'd cooked up and feed it to someone else. Distance themselves from the threat and get a better story out of it, to boot.

They needed a soldier, and here I was.

×

The beginning, at least, was all worked out beforehand. I would accompany the Congressman into Banquet Room C as an official representative of the hotel. My stated role was to cover the Congressman while he took down the bear, and to intervene only in the event of an emergency. I was issued a shotgun, a Remington 870 pump-action twelve-gauge, personally delivered by a VP from the GamePro Outfitters Group of Companies, who had generously offered to provide whatever aid they could to help end the crisis. The manager got the local TV news to film me holding the gun with my arm around the GamePro rep, who joked about how it was the best choice for getting lead into a bear that was coming at you with a chip on its shoulder. I thought about asking for protective clothing but gave up on the idea as soon as the manager stepped in and thanked GamePro for the donation of this excellent weapon, saying how the Royal Oak was a place that had a long and dignified tradition of service and of course I'd be perfectly safe in my trademark bellhop uniform, which was emblematic of the hotel's commitment to quality. After all, the Congressman was wearing nothing but a western button-up, a leather vest and a pair of old Levi's — regular-person clothes — so why should I expect preferential treatment? Taking the cue, I pushed my bellhop's cap to a rakish angle before shaking the manager's hand to seal our contract for the cameras.

The media would be allowed to stay in the lobby to report on the operation, but for obvious safety and insurance reasons, no cameras could accompany us into the banquet room. *Grizzly down; all clear!* would be the signal that we'd achieved our objective and that it was safe to open the doors.

Bow-legged, the Congressman led the approach. I flanked him on the left. The hotel manager followed to shut the doors behind us. At the threshold, the Congressman paused, took off his vest, unholstered his Colt, and gave a little wave and a yip to the cameras, to scattered applause.

As soon as we stepped into the banquet room, everything got quiet. The stink of the bear was everywhere—piss and shit and fur and woods, the musk of a creature that had no business being within the walls of the hotel, within any walls. The Congressman had dropped back so that we were shoulder to shoulder, and I could smell the fear coming off him, too, the eggy stink leaching out under his cologne. He was walking in a crouch and holding his gun at a downward angle, as though he'd forgotten it was there and what it was for. If I'd barked at him then, I think he would have shat himself. Instead, I asked in a low voice if he'd locked on the target.

In the far corner of the room, in a nook behind the stage drapes, the bear sat, squat and huge amid stacks of red plush chairs, pawing at a lectern it had knocked on its side. Its fur was bristled and greying around the neck. Its eyes were beady and black. In its size and strength and capacity for damage, it was a monster. But as the Congressman remembered the pistol in his hands and raised it to take aim, the thing just looked dumbly back, as though it simply wanted fish and couldn't imagine why none were available, or how the river from which it drew its meat had disappeared—but understood, instinctually, that its fate was beyond its control.

From where we stood, the shot was too long, and the Congressman knew it. He looked back at me, expectant, and I gestured to stay low and move in toward the bear, to take cover behind the dining tables scattered around the room. He nodded, cocked the hammer of his gun and put a grim look on his face.

"Let's show this motherfucker who's boss," he said, though his stammering gave him away.

He grunted as he crept forward. I stayed behind him, shotgun ready, wondering how fast the bear could spring to life and barrel across the room and break both of our necks with a swipe of its mitt. Grizzlies aren't typically aggressive animals, unless they feel threatened. But you can't really tame them. The chances of a cornered one lashing out and committing casual murder are high. This one stayed put, though, prying splinters from the lectern, its head lolling back and forth. We crept from table to table to take up a shielded position around twenty paces from the bear. It didn't so much as snuffle in our direction. It was only when the Congressman rose with his back straight and held out his Colt with both hands—and just stood there, shaking, while seconds ticked past—that it finally looked over at us, raised a paw to swat at the lectern, and gave a stupefied roar.

When the Congressman's knees buckled, I knew. He collapsed back behind the table, his whole body quaking. The fear was like jaundice on his face, yellow, inflamed.

"I can't," he said. "I can't."

"Have you ever shot anything before? *Sir?*"

"We're not looking at a fucking duck, are we? Goddamn it, son!"

Whatever he summoned then to convince himself must be that quality all important men possess, which allows them to focus without distraction on the absolute present, their certainty distilled so its purity can't be questioned when others are asked to drink of its cup. That, or it was just the potency of his fear—some rarefied version of the bone-shaking terror I'd known so intimately that this face off with a cornered grizzly played like an exercise, a routine chore.

"Look, we all understand our roles here tonight," the Congressman said, and held out the Colt. I gestured at the shotgun. The Congressman waggled the Colt at me and said, "No, it can't go down like that." I took the heavy old piece that it was known he wouldn't even let his wife touch, and stood to take a bead on the grizzly.

I wanted so much for it to stand up. I wished for it, *willed* it, to get indignant and extend to its full height, flash its teeth and pound its chest and charge me at full run. I took a few steps toward it, sights lined up right in the corner of its glassy eye. The damn thing didn't move. The urban environment had cloaked its senses like a burlap cowl; mentally, it was lost somewhere among the ghosts of brothers and sisters fumbling through phantom woods, a weightless echo of the real ones it had been torn from and knew it would never see again. The grizzly understood that it was alone, and that the creatures who'd brought it here did not wish it well.

I would say that's what allowed me to do it, finally — the anger I felt that, after its burst of terrified rage, this fearsome thing had become so useless, so neutered and disoriented by the environment of the hotel, that it stopped knowing how to defend itself. That it had ended up in such a stupid situation, such a mighty beast so easily brought low by human pride.

I would say that — except that I would have killed it anyway. As it happened, it just took a little less effort.

In fact, I had no trouble at all walking ten paces and planting two quick shots into its face, one into each eye, the expansion bullets taking the whole crown off the skull and throwing fur-flecked bone and pink splatter all over the velvet stage curtains. Once the bear had slumped over in its mess, I put another round into its heart, to stop it from twitching. I knew the animal was dead — knew well enough what dead looked like — but for good measure I leaned over and held my hand in front of its nose to make sure the breath was gone. The smells of sulphur and metal and gamey blood filled my nose, and I thought, as I often had, how it was all the same — bears or warriors or children, all just a tangle of pink meat and brittle bone under a thinness of pleading skin.

Turning from the bear, I saw the Congressman standing where I'd left him, hands clutching the lip of the upturned table, looking at me with something like hatred. The ruddy tone had returned to his jaw and his chin had stopped trembling. Righteousness was gathering in his eyes like a thundercloud. He couldn't stand it — the ways in which he needed me, and did not. He couldn't tolerate how expendable I was, how useful and anonymous and effective. There was still fear in his look, too, and I knew that while he hated me, he was also afraid of me—as many others had been, and been right to be.

We faced each other for a few seconds. I had both guns, and the guts of a dead bear spattered on my uniform. The Congressman had nothing on his person but a sweaty Egyptian cotton shirt. Yet his very presence in that room represented the huge apparatus he wore like armor: the connections and money, the reputation, the assumption of authority that came with his US passport, the potency of belief in his providence. I didn't even make him ask—what good would it have done? I couldn't imagine my situation being better than it was. Sara had been clear about that: I was being given a second, maybe even third chance to start fresh, working a steady job for an iconic hotel. A service position, and rightly so: I was nothing if not trained to serve. That was how it was, for men like me.

I walked over to the Congressman and handed him the Colt. "Two in the eyes, and one in the heart," I said. He took the gun and nodded and gestured for me to take my place behind him on the left. I did so without comment.

"Grizzly down!" he shouted, the confidence returned to his voice, the zeal of the preacher. "*All clear!*"

× × ×

The famous photo from that day shows the Congressman and the hotel manager in Banquet Room C, shaking hands in front of the carcass, visibly pleased at how they'd managed to avert the crisis, save the dignity of an historic landmark, and prove what you could accomplish when all the waffling stopped and you just let people do what they did best, be it a question of varmints or pipelines. I knew enough to stand back as the TV crews crowded in, the two men stepping up to field questions while I hugged the shadows, trying to fade into the background.

Likewise, you'll find no credit underneath the grizzly's head, which is still hanging in the hotel lobby, mounted over the main staircase, ruined skull and all. There's not even a mention of my role—and of that I'm not sorry. It only became clear later on that it was one of the last bears of its kind, and I'd want no curse nor accolade I might receive if my part in finishing off that once-feared species were more widely known. It's enough that now, when I speak of my past, I can tell this story—of how the grizzly came to hang here, a testament to the sad appetites of powerful men—and not speak of my other past, the one I spent so long trying to lose.

Neutral Buoyancy

The others always make it harder to achieve results.

Kielbasa Joe perches on a foam noodle folded under his paunch, paddling up the fourth lane at the speed of a bored sea slug, the fluorescent poolroom lights making his skin look blanched and sausage-like. There's no sense waiting for him; he'll hog the lane for a full hour, noodling back and forth without a twinge of shame. Likewise, Doctor O.C.D. Grumblestein is busy evenly spacing the lane markers along the rope of lane five, muttering the whole time like he always does, as though that qualifies as exercise; that's probably a twenty-minute wait. Which leaves Chatty Boners chatting up one of his AquaTramps in lanes two and three, and Wady Mary, doing her wady dance in the shallow end of lane one, the flotation belt cinched around her waist propping up her saggy tits like beached jellyfish.

For Jetta, this is probably the best option, because not only does Wady Mary get tired quickly, she also buckles under pressure. So she'll probably give up her lane as soon as Jetta goes over and stands at the head of it, doing stretches, to communicate as emphatically as she can without yelling out loud that if there isn't a free lane by 1:15 p.m., which is exactly four minutes from now, she'll just dive in and dart past Wady Mary underwater like a tadpole. Just another challenge, she thinks, to incorporate into her daily sixty. Another test of her resilience.

Sixty laps, every day, for the past three years: this is the constant by which Jetta Crisp runs her life. Every day at the BeWell Downtown pool, in by 1:15 p.m., out by 2. This is the ritual, no matter what; her health depends on it. Swimming is the best exercise, full-body with therapeutic stress-reduction benefits. She has no intention of missing a day and breaking her streak, even with her job as busy as ever; in fact this is exactly why she absolutely has to get started by 1:15 or risk overshooting her lunch break and having to stay an extra hour in the evening.

Strength in routine, her doctor said, equates to strength in the body. Sixty a day to keep relapse at bay. Toughen up your sinews enough to keep the lymphoma gone for good.

So Jetta takes her position and begins her stretching, swinging her arms up in a huge arc to make sure Wady Mary gets the picture. Sure enough, with the first sun salutation, the old woman smiles weakly at her and climbs out of the pool at the speed of a tortoise, every creaky step making Jetta's heart rate shoot up another notch. *Getoutgetoutgetout,* she thinks. She can feel her veins winching up inside her, making her whole body rigid, the perfunctory yoga not helping at all, her heart flapping under her rib cage like a panicked fish. For a second it feels like the woman will never get out, like she'll just freeze there on the shallow stairs, dripping chlorinated drips down her tapioca-pudge thighs until Jetta sun-salutates herself into an aneurism and her head explodes all over the pool room.

Then she's in, and everything softens.

The water welcomes her like a gentle confessor, the hard slappy echoes of the tiled room melting away in the warm, soothing ripples. Jetta's breathing slows to deep, even waves. She pulls a silicone swim cap over her close-cropped hair, puts on her goggles, and gives a sideways glance over at the other swimmers, all the ones she's named for their faults, the ways in which they're not as serious about this as she is, the things they keep trying to improve on, even though they always fail. Sometimes, once she's gotten a lane and there's no more doubt about whether she'll make her sixty that day, she begins to feel a bit bad about mocking these people so mercilessly in her head. The old and overweight and lonely. The ones here just for something to do. They sometimes speak to each other—Chatty

Boners spends most of his time in the pool jabbering away, trying to pick up whatever damp floozy has taken the lane beside him that day—but Jetta never talks to them. She treasures the pool as a silent space. On her program, there's no time for inane chatter or pointless conversation or mundane stresses, the kind of aimless, insignificant stuff she assumes these people talk about.

Too much guilt, though, too much anxiety: these cause her to lose time and focus, and that's not an option. The BeWell slogans are there on the wall to remind her, painted in bright orange above the life preserver:

Focus on your Goal and Achieve Results
BE THE BEST POSSIBLE YOU

This is not about other people. This is about wellness, transformation, and survival.

So: breathe in, go under, and launch. Jetta fires forward, dolphin-kicking for six seconds, feeling her skin and muscles coalesce with the water. This is what she yearns for, this dissolution of boundaries, this neutralizing liquefaction. She kicks up toward the light and gets into her steady crawl, stroke, stroke, breathe; stroke, stroke, breathe; legs straight and fluttering, palms cupped closed and pulling the water so she can feel her deltoids work, trying to move with the sleek, fluid grace of a dolphin. Once Jetta is away, there's no stopping the motion, no pausing in the pursuit of her daily sixty: twenty front, twenty back, twenty butterfly. She waits for the moment she loves most of all, when she finds exactly the right velocity of breath, exhaling in the water to create tiny, perfect bubbles, so that when she turns her head her intake is expertly timed to coincide with the machinelike motion of her limbs, splash-burble-splash-burble-inhale. Inside and outside, working in concert. Fully cetaceous. Uncorrupted. Alive.

Only when she rears up to turn over for one of her nimble porpoise-flips does the pool room come back to her, with its plastic couches and bleary skylights seeping grey, filtered light. But now that she's become the water, she doesn't need these things in order to see. To *know*. She can feel in the fluctuations of her blood, the ebb and flow of the swimmers as they vacate the pool, how the water calms when Kielbasa Joe stops his noodling and climbs out, and Chatty Boners follows, taking his pursuit of the red-headed pool nymph into the sauna area. Jetta loves it best when she has the pool all to herself, but it's not so bad if Dr. O.C.D. Grumblestein and his arthritic pacing are all she has to tune out to get into the Zone — the place where her thoughts actually stop, and she's nothing but pure liquid energy. Jetta has only 11 per cent body fat (Marie at work, who's overweight, is always telling her she can see Jetta's spine poking out from under her blouse, but Dr. Grice says that's just how her structure is now), but when she gets into the Zone it's like she weighs zero, no more malignant tissue, no more infected marrow. *Keep moving*, she thinks. *Leave it behind.*

She's flying now, knocking off laps with total ease, feeling the Zone open up before her like a blowhole in the fluid molecules of the water.

Eighteen... nineteen... twenty... flip!

Now she's on her back, following the seams of the tiled ceiling to keep straight, closing her eyes once she feels the alignment, her muscles knowing the proper trajectory.

Twenty-four... twenty-five...

Jetta opens her eyes to check the ceiling in case, and a splash plumes up somewhere beside her. It's not like Dr. Grumblestein to stir things up. Usually he's strictly a water walker, maybe a few foam weights here and there, never anything approaching a proper stroke. So Jetta's irritated that on the one day when he's the only other swimmer, he's decided to go spazzy.

But she's in the Zone now, really almost really in it, so she can't think about it too much. *Focus on your Goal and Achieve Results. BE THE BEST POSSIBLE YOU.*

Thirty-two . . . thirty-three . . .

Thing is, it doesn't stop. Although Jetta tries to keep her stroke as aerodynamic as possible, gliding through water to cause the least possible friction, she can feel little droplets of pool spume landing on her face from Dr. Grumblestein's water-mosh.

Thirty-eight . . . thirty-nine . . . flip!

As she turns and pushes off the wall to start the final leg of her sixty—butterfly stroke, the toughest and most addictive of all—she sees. The splashing in lane five isn't controlled. There's no rhythm or logic to it. Could be Dr. Grumblestein is throwing a fit, and how could she blame him? But then she hears him call out, and knows that's not it.

Forty-four . . . forty-five . . .

Dr. Grumblestein is in trouble. But she has to keep going, because she's almost in the Zone but also glanced at the clock and it's pushing 2:55 and if she stops to help him now, she won't finish.

Sixty laps a day, every day, for the past three years. Jetta Crisp keeps lunging through the water, achieving as hard as she can, hurtling like a shimmer of reflected light toward the moment when she can touch the wall and stop swimming and come back to real time and go help the old man. Pushes herself to go harder, faster, finishing sooner, even though she hates it so much—the moment when she stops, and her body comes back to her in all its earthbound weakness. Hates the old man's body, too, for screaming its failure at her through her precious amniotic veil.

Forty-eight . . . forty-nine . . .

She can see him beneath the water, now, whenever she plunges her head under for another stroke. Where there's supposed to be no one else in the world, just pure achievement, there he is: spewing bubbles, knee twisted in a gruesome kink, eyes aghast and bulging in the chlorinated blear.

Fifty...fifty-one...

She knows he can see her, and that she's the only one who can save him. The attendants at the front desk never watch the pool-room video feed, and by now it would take them too long to get up the stairs and into the pool, anyway, because he's already starting to turn the same blue as the water that's smothering him.

She wishes, wishes so hard, that she could become water. Indifferent. Antiseptic. Solvent, and absolving.

As she swerves, a chemical mouthful fills her lungs. She swallows it, stifling coughs and dolphin-kicking hard under the lane markers until she's on top of him. She hauls at his weight, pushing his head above the surface, clutching his limp arm while she clambers, all bones and angles, onto the deck. She tugs it as hard as she can to get Dr. Grumblestein up onto the tile, his body far more solid than its papery skin makes it look, and clamps her hands over his chest and pushes, one-two-three, one-two-three, then plugs his nose and locks her mouth onto his, blowing out whatever air she has left, blowing all her energy and momentum into his lungs to send a jolt to his heart, filling him with her Zone, until he sputters out white froth and inhales a big, desperate gulp of air and starts breathing again.

×

The worst is that he forgave her.

Jetta turns the hot water up until it's steaming. She's standing in the shower, quaking, trying to convince herself she didn't just almost let a man drown.

After he came to, she'd just sat there on the tile, crying, saying, "I'm sorry, I'm sorry, I was in the Zone." And between gurgling breaths he'd put his hand on her tricep and said, "It's okay. Don't cry, don't cry. I'm alive, thanks to you." He even called her a hero when the attendants finally realized what was happening and came barrelling into the pool room, rescue buoys at the ready, blowing stupidly into their whistles, as though that would help anything. Then later, when she said she had to excuse herself and get back to work, when she scuttled away like a wet rat, reeking with shame, he'd held out his hand and said, "I'm John," and the first thing she'd thought was, *No, no, I can't know your name, because now how will I swim? How will I swim now?*

The water hits her skin, scalding and hard, stripping away in pressurized heat the last few calories she's retained by missing her sixty for the first time in three years. She folds her arms over her tiny breasts, pushing them down into her rib cage, feeling echoes of the lymphoma whispering in her cells, leans against the slick shower wall and lets her face twist into whatever horrified and broken shape it wants—trying to leach it out, that moment when she saw him drowning and thought, *Maybe it wouldn't be so bad.* Maybe it wouldn't be such a bad thing at all, to sink to the bottom and fill with water, and be still.

Home Range

She is tiny and thin, maybe six, wearing a white blouse smudged with grease and oil, and a navy skirt that barely covers her scraped knees. When Kyle hauls up the door she's just standing there like a curious bird, dead still, echoes of the metal's clang circling her like nervous black cats half-hidden in the shadows. The sight of her inside the container, amid the stacked pallets and crates smelling of wet tin and briny mildew, is like a lullaby lilted over a pounding hardcore beat, incongruous and adorable and unsettling as hell.

It takes Kyle three seconds to realize he can't tell anyone about the girl, five to figure out he can't just leave her there, ten to know how fucked he is as a result. Fifteen to write it off as just more of the cursed luck that's his trademark, as much a token of his being as the sleeve tattoos that fill both his arms from shoulder to wrist with a chaos of thorny blue vines.

He looks around the empty pier. The Atlantic sloshes and gurgles, the sound answered by the croaking of gulls and the grinding of heavy machinery behind him. Pier 17 is out on the far edge of the wharf, rows of lots away from the main office and the warehousing deck. It's just him and his forklift and the sludge of trash and seaweed slapping the breaker wall. And the girl. Japanese, maybe. No. More likely poorer, easier to make disappear. Thai or Malaysian, something like that. Fuck knows. Wherever she's come from, she's far from home, and Kyle is willing to bet his signed vinyl copy of *Jane Doe* that the trip wasn't her choice.

He curses in his head, cycling through options at blastbeat pace, *whattodowhattodowhattodo.*

"Speak English?" he says. No response. "Name? What's your name?" The girl just looks at him, head cocked to one side, hiding with quizzical calm whatever explosions of terror and confusion must be raging in her brain like Bengal flares.

"Fuck," he says, to no one. The wind tickles his nose with gull shit, wood rot, and tar slag. In the distance he hears the bleating reverse alarm of another forklift, the harmonic whirr of the hydraulic elevator. Even out here at 17, he has ten, maybe fifteen minutes before someone drives by, grunt or foreman, to ask what the fuck is taking him so long with the shipment from Kwai Tsing.

In the end it's maybe a two-minute decision, based on what's immediately available, proximity to the parking lot, number of hours left in his shift. All instinct, like the survival games he used to play as a kid. If there's anything Kyle can say he's good at, it's surviving.

There's a big roll of brown packing paper leaning against a nearby stack of crates. He gestures to the girl: *Come out.* She steps slowly from the container, blinking in the salt mist. Kyle notices the bruising on her arms. She's probably spent her whole trip, from Asia through the Suez and the Mediterranean, in total darkness, cowering in a far corner of the container. If anyone's checked on her, it sure as hell hasn't been to offer comfort.

He wonders what she's been eating, if he should check the interior for evidence — wrappers, crumbs, some kind of bed. Not that it matters. Whoever shipped her knows which lot she's in and will have carefully traced its route from Hong Kong to 17. The TP11 Eastbound route is a forty-day trip, at best. There's no way she could have gotten this far without a network of people making it happen. There'll be handlers waiting. A buyer, with expectations and a lot of money on the line. Valuable cargo, this.

It's a freak chance, a big mistake, that Kyle's the one here on the receiving end. So he doesn't have time to work out the consequences: it has to be fast, brutal, full-on. Instinct over thought.

Maybe, he thinks for the millionth time, he isn't done with punk rock yet. Maybe he can save her.

Drawing out a large swath of the paper, he wraps it round the girl, placing his hand gently on the crown of her head to keep her still and try to communicate that he's trying to help, until she's just an inconspicuous brown sausage, another bit of material piled on the back platform of his Caterpillar. He makes sure she's on her back, has a slit to breathe through. Does what he can to tell her to keep still. She gives no pushback. Before folding the flap down over her head to hide her smooth black hair, he leans in and whispers to her, shitting his pants, patting his chest, "Friend. Friend. Home. My home. *Konichiwa?*" A bit of packing tape and she's invisible.

Hour and a half until quitting. Finish your tasks, don't look anyone in the face, park the lift, haul her out like an old carpet or a bit of excess wrap for dumping, throw her in the back seat of the pickup, drive home without speeding. Get her inside. Between now and then, he figures, he can sort out what the fuck he's going to tell Abby.

×

They sit on the worn turquoise carpet, playing. Most of Abby's dolls have missing limbs and torn clothes, but she still manages to craft amazing mini-luxe fantasies with them: shopping, eating at fancy restaurants, driving around astride the old Tonka truck Kyle picked up at the Sally Ann. The language barrier is less of a problem for kids. The Asian girl — he's resisted giving her a name — took no time to warm up to the dolls. She obviously knows Barbie. She and Abby are busy placing them in pairs, with their thin plastic legs stretched out, feet touching.

He thinks how much Krista would have loved this. She always said she wanted two.

It will be six years in November. It'd be impossible to forget anyway, but the anniversary coming a day after Abby's birthday always makes for a particularly bad emotional thrashing. He still has trouble believing it. Sepsis doesn't seem like a thing that should kill people, not in this country, not in this age. Not at barely twenty-four years old, with skin thickened to the toughness of steel by a lifetime of fighting to convince people that you're more than your bleached hair, your piercings, and your poisoned history. Kris had already been through hell by the time she met Kyle—gropey father, drunk mom, more than a few winter nights sleeping on the street. That she'd managed to pull herself up, find the strength to help others through her work at the shelter: it was a miracle. She only got the one, though. Unless you also count Abby, the child she knew for a day and a half. Kris never even made it home from the hospital.

The girls are keeping busy for now, so Kyle gives himself a minute to sit on the couch and work up a plan. Normally he'd put on a record to help him think, *I Against I* or *Monuments to Thieves*, but he doesn't want to scare the new girl with the noise he loves. Instead he turns on the TV and clicks around until he finds a station rerunning *The Shawshank Redemption*. Vanilla as it is, Kyle has a soft spot for the movie. He'd convinced his old band, Pinched Nerve, to name a song after it—"Andy Dufresne." Krista had always loved that one, made sure to come up close to the stage whenever they played it, to watch him shred through the blitzkrieg chorus: *"He says there's no memory / I want to live what's left of my life / In a warm place / Without memory."* Her smiling, arms raised, screaming along with him, feeling the same ache.

He'll have to keep the girl here for tonight, at least. He knows it can't go much beyond that. An orphanage, maybe? The thought chills him, all wrought iron beds and sadistic nurses and gruel. Besides, what's he going to do—leave her on the doorstep, tied with ribbon? Rewrap her in the packing paper and call it an early Christmas parcel? He wants her to be safe, protected, but there can't be anything linking her to him. With the band long finished, the wharf is his lifeline now. Abby will be starting school next fall, which means books, clothes, backpacks. Things to pay for.

He opens a couple cans of Beefaroni for the girls and gives them another half hour of play before taking them together into the washroom. Abby picks up her toothbrush and squirts on a blob of bubblegum-flavoured toothpaste.

"Daddy, is it okay if Soo-bin and I share?" she says.

For a second he hears *soy bean*. Then he realizes. Winces. Nods his head.

"Yes, sweetie."

The girl—Soo-bin—takes the brush, touches it to the stream of water from the tap, and runs it back and forth across her little Chiclet teeth, curious and mute. He wonders how much of this is new to her, what kind of conditions she lived in back home. He wonders if she feels lucky that Kyle found her. He wonders if she is.

Once the girls are asleep, he sits down in front of *Shawshank* with a can of Pabst to decompress. He goes through the exercises his mother taught him after Kris died: start with the eyes. Then the jaw. Move down through the neck and shoulders. Let relaxation fall over your joints like dandelion wisps. He still finds himself fighting it—answering every loosening with a desire to grit teeth, grip mic, bark a righteous retort. Pummel stress into submission. Live hard-core as a steady inner scream.

There's no one to scream at, though. Just Red and Andy Dufresne, and why would he scream at them. He swigs beer, savouring the sour aluminum fizz. Closes his eyes, trying to feel the warm place.

Kris, massaging his shoulders after a show. Working the strained muscle, popping a joint into his mouth from behind, holding it for him while he inhales.

Over the droning of the TV, he hears a dull thump outside. His eyes pop open. The girl? He gets up, drains his beer, and goes over to peer through the half-open door to Abby's room. Two bundles snuggle each other on the bed, rising and falling with children's breath. Safe, both. He turns back to the movie, where Andy Dufresne is counting seconds between thunderclaps. Kyle doubts anyone from the wharf would come for him at night. Not worth the effort, when you can intimidate someone just as well in the light of day.

He hears the hollow clunk again. Recognizes tactile, insistent scratching. This part of town is a magnet for raccoons. He grabs the broom and another Pabst and snaps the porch light on before stepping out into the foggy, grey night.

Crouched comfortably on its haunches amid a chaos of apple cores and cheese-caked pizza boxes, nibbling away at the remains of an old corn cob, the fat masked invader squats in front of the upturned bin and turns its head toward Kyle: *What? What you gonna do?* Kyle waves the broom around a few times, smacks it on the paint-chipped porch slats. He knows it's futile. These things have no fear, will sit there ransacking your trash right in front of you unless you take drastic measures. Kyle's never had the heart. Krista volunteered at the humane society and would always come home with horror stories about coons full of buckshot, or choking their way through the last throes of death by Javex-brined chicken carcass. For the most part, he's learned to live with them, clean up their toxic feces during the day, and hope they end up moving on to another bin once they've had their fill of the meagre leavings in his.

Besides, Kyle and the raccoons go back a ways. He remembers a night his grandfather let him help set the traps. Non-lethal — just a bit of peanut butter bait and a trigger-action wire-mesh door that would hold them until morning, when Granddad would load the cage in the back of his pickup and drive them outside the city limits to let them free. Kyle wanted to know why he couldn't just put them in the neighbour's yard.

"Thing about raccoons," said his grandfather. "They know where they live. Know their territory. You gotta take 'em an hour out at least, go out beyond their home range. Otherwise, they'll just come back."

Kyle stares at the big mangy guy gnawing the cob like an old man chewing on a pipe stem. He wonders if this critter has been here before. If he recognizes Kyle—knows that this thin, wiry ex-punk with the two-day stubble and bramble tats is no threat to him. Kyle can smell his musk, the sour stink of old fish and muddy water. The raccoon keeps nibbling, eyes cast sideways at Kyle, waiting for him finally to get angry and take a real swing with the broom.

Kyle turns and goes inside and clicks off the porch light. White credits crawl up the black screen, hundreds of names disappearing as they crest the dusty curve of his old tube TV. Kyle clicks off the remote and the room plunges into darkness. He listens, for a minute, to make sure he can still hear the girls breathing, before going into his bedroom and collapsing into his unmade bed with his jeans on.

×

The knock comes at ten a.m., as the girls are tucking into their Quaker Maple & Brown Sugar Instant Oatmeal. Even though he's been waiting for it, Kyle flinches like he's been stuck with a shiv up under the ribs. He spent all night thinking, trying to sort out what to do with the girl—with Soo-bin. But he just kept coming back to Andy Dufresne, hammering on his sewage pipe in the darkness, and to Krista, lying on the hospital bed, the berserking metronome of the heart monitor shocking her life into the terrible flatline that took all of Kyle's rage and pinched it into the helpless scream of a newborn. And to Abigail, *his daughter, his daughter, his daughter,* the word so charged with joy and pain that it still explodes, every time he thinks it, like a bomb inside the chambers of his scar-worn heart.

The next knock comes, more insistent than the first. He gets up and gives himself maybe thirty seconds to haul Soo-bin up out of her kitchen chair, shushing Abby to quell her hurt questioning look, and hauls the cargo girl into his bedroom, where he stuffs her into the closet and puts all the compassion he has into his eyes and mumbles an apologetic plea—*justaminutepleasebequietjustaminute*—before piling an old Slayer hoodie on top of her and closing the door and heading back out to answer to whoever it is that wants her back. As he grips the knob, Kyle puts on his calmest face, thinking how natural it will be to pretend that the second bowl of Quaker was for himself, hoping for the absurd impossibility that somehow, instead of someone from the union, it's the raccoon from last night come knocking to ask him for another corn cob, or to apologize for the awkward standoff they'd found themselves in during the midnight raid.

"Mr. Miller. Good morning."

Kyle's fantasy falls away as soon as he opens the door and sees Szandor Szabados, head of the local ILA chapter, standing there with his cigarette pinched daintily between thumb and forefinger, shoulders hunched into his thick khaki coat, eyes gleaming oily crow-black under a thinning fringe of copper-pipe hair. Kyle has seen Szandor berate his fair share of stevedores, but that's just the tip of it. Rumours have him deeply involved in trafficking, graft, and pedophilia, and they're the kind of rumours everyone knows are true. Szabados keeps one can of Diet Pepsi per day in the staff refrigerator. Kyle remembers the day some rookie decided to drink it and ended up getting a pink slip and a six-foot-five, 270-pound escort to the parking lot, who made it crystal clear that any further appearance at the wharf would result in a dislocated jaw and the distinct possibility of an indelicately removed testicle.

"Szandor?" Kyle says, feigning surprise, trying to channel his old performer's instincts. "Surprised to see you on my porch on a Saturday morning. Can I do for you?"

Szabados takes a long drag of his cigarette and looks sideways down the street, in the direction of the ocean.

"You want to come in?" says Kyle, stepping slightly to the side, hoping to hell the answer is no.

"I got a bit of a problem, Miller," Szabados says. "Maybe you can help me."

"Sure."

"You were on 17 yesterday, yeah?"

"That's right."

Szabados looks him in the eye, a barrel of smouldering ash clinging to the tip of his butt. "I know it is. I know you were on 17."

Kyle manages a curious frown. "What's the problem?"

"You see anything unusual on your shift?"

"No...can't say I did."

"Can't say? Or...?"

Kyle tries to summon saliva into his mouth, which suddenly feels coated with cement.

"I honestly don't know what you're getting at. Sorry to disappoint. Yesterday was a pretty standard shift."

Szabados chucks his smoke onto the worn planks of Kyle's porch, not far from the dark smears left from the raccoon's marauding. He shoves his hands deep into his pockets, looks back down the road, presenting Kyle with a gnarled cauliflower ear veined through with red blood vessels.

"All right, Miller," he says. "Just remember. The union's here to take care of you. I know you like your days off to spend with your daughter."

Kyle says nothing.

"Be sure to let me know if you hear anything on the wharf, yeah?"

"Okay, Szandor. Will do."

"Me, I'm gonna go get some lunch. Great little Korean place up near Fairmount," he says. "You like Korean?"

For a minute Kyle is confused, thinks this evil gnome might actually be asking him out for a meal.

"I love it," Szabados says. "Even that kimchi. Smells like an old sock. You gotta watch the spice, though. You're not careful, it can wreak havoc on your insides."

The implication jabs a stinger at Kyle's brain, prodding for the name that's suddenly shaking inside him like a trembling kitten: *Soo-bin.*

Like Korean, Kyle?

Szabados turns to go, but stops and twists his head around, demon-style, at the bottom of Kyle's steps.

"Anything pops into your head, anyone call you with something to talk about, you remember — the union takes care of you." He fishes in his pocket, pulls out a flattened pack of Kools, draws one out, and starts tapping it on the inside of his wrist. "Remember that."

"Will do, Szandor."

"See you at work."

Kyle watches Szandor Szabados get into his big black Escalade, shut the door, and drive off in the opposite direction of Fairmount, most likely back to the wharf, to retrieve his voodooed Pepsi from its shelf in the staff fridge. Kyle thinks about what's in his own closet, about Abby and her oatmeal, the other bowl cold and congealing beside her. He thinks about Andy Dufresne, keeping his eye on the warm place with no memory. And he thinks about Krista, because he's always thinking about her.

×

"Where are you going, Daddy?"

The question scuttles back and forth across the dome of his skull, mewling. Abby had known something was weird, of course: Saturdays were their together day, the one put aside to forget bank accounts and old music and dead mothers and the clawing of freighter exhaust in the back of your throat. When he'd taken Abby next door to Mrs. Coover's to plead the favour of watching her for a couple hours, his daughter had been smart or scared enough not to mention Soo-bin. He'd told Abby that he was going to help the girl get home, and she'd accepted that. But she still required some answer for his absence, a good reason for his leaving her with the neighbour on a Saturday evening.

The truth would have meant nothing to her. Wharton State Forest, just north of Atlantic City, isn't somewhere she knows. In fact, it's far enough in the wrong direction that Kyle hopes it's a place she'll never end up. He tries not to pressure Abby, to be patient and careful with her. But he's definitely pointing her outside the state— across the river, maybe. Or even farther—north, to a saner country. If he has any say in the matter, the whole south shore of New Jersey will exist outside her universe, just not something she'll have to live with, not the way he does.

The Korean girl—North Korean, is Kyle's guess, almost a ghost to begin with—shifts in the passenger seat, staring out the window at the strip malls and industrial parks running along the edge of the turnpike. The cabin smells of stale coffee and sweat and Cheetos and Armor All, which together Kyle processes as the reek of his own helplessness and guilt.

Wharton is big, big enough for someone to get lost in. To go unnoticed. But also a place, maybe, where someone small but resourceful might find a way to survive. It's only the beginning of November. Kyle's leaving Soo-bin with Abby's Barbie parka from last season—a bit tight, but warm—some plaid galoshes, a pair of track pants, and an old sweater of Krista's that's big enough for her to wrap around herself like a blanket. To eat, a bunch of bananas, a couple packages of Fig Newtons, and a Thermos of instant hot chocolate. It's a far cry from a proper wilderness-survival kit, but surely better than what Szandor Szabados had planned for her.

He couldn't bring himself to call the cops. One way or the other, they'd have involved Szabados. Some of them are probably on his payroll. Besides, if Kyle's honest with himself, he's already, technically, kidnapped the girl. What else might they say he'd done? What horrible mix of tar and feathers and bird shit could they smear all over him? The orphanage appears in his head again, rows of metal-frame beds and hard-edged shadows, but this time it's Abby standing there, dressed in a grey smock, surrounded by faceless orphans. Her mother dead. Her father convicted. Maybe dead, too.

He's trying. Trying so hard. With the Chef Boyardee and the oatmeal and the thrift store dolls. Processed shit, material shit—the kind of shit he used to rage against. It's all he can afford now, though. You make sacrifices. Kyle wants Abby to have a good life with him, and a decent shot at a better one down the road. He can't shatter that chance. Not for anyone. Not after what he promised.

✕

In the hospital, Krista's just lying there. The oxygen mask makes it hard for Kyle to hear her, and there's a noise in his head like a thousand bands slamming through a frenzied breakdown, all shredded vocal cords and shrill guitar and kick-drum hammering. He's squeezing Kris's hand, hard, but his other hand is up on her forearm, wrapped around the blue ring of barbed wire tattooed on her bicep, not squeezing as tightly there because he knows her skin is tender. Abby is with the nurses. There will be a little more time for mother and daughter to be in the same room—they've promised her that—but the doctors don't like having the baby in the ICU. Kris has already had one kidney fail. They've stopped telling him she'll get better.

She's made it clear that she needs him to listen carefully. It's hard for her to talk now, so Kyle leans in and puts his ear over the cup of the oxygen mask.

"You have to promise," she whispers, a cracked cymbal rasp, shattered and terrified and brave, so brave. "You'll take care of her."

"I will," Kyle says, shaking. "I promise." He can't imagine how he'll do this without Krista. He can't believe what's happening. He can't believe he can't save her. The bands explode in his head into a final pummelling unison, and he recognizes the opening bars of "Last Light," first song proper on Converge's *You Fail Me*, his favourite track on the record, which he's been listening to a lot lately.

"Always," Kyle says, his voice breaking.

"It's going to mean giving up some things," Kris says.

"I know," he says, blood clanging in his ears, a righteous screaming wounded animal roar. "I know."

×

He turns onto a dark road that winds up through wooded slopes. The trees are thick on either side. The lake is just up around the bend about two hundred yards. He pulls over into a clearing, kills the engine and the headlights. The air is crisp and clean, and there's a faint scent of woodsmoke on the wind and a burbling brook nearby. He climbs out, his breath steaming in the cold, and opens the back door. He unbuckles her seatbelt and steps back and—hating himself for it—waves his hand.

"C'mon, Soo-bin."

She climbs out into the night, boots crunching on the brown leaves.

He squats and looks her in the eyes—big eyes, dark as tea in a black cup. There are fortunes there, tellings beyond what he has the ability to read. This, finally, is his problem: What else can he do for her? How does she fit? How is she at all comprehensible? The truth—*I want to save her, she reminds me of my daughter, but I can't, I can't risk it, because she is not my daughter*—is too banal, too horrible for Kyle to contemplate. Justice? Where? In what universe does she get handed over to anyone else, anyone good, and not draw all kinds of attention, some politician using her as a campaign platform, some cynical commentator preaching the girl's plight as a harbinger of moral decay? How does that not all boil down to himself and to Abby?

And does Soo-bin even end up any better off? In what scenario is she most likely to be free, really free, for as long as possible?

Kyle can give her the chance to run, to adapt. It's the best act of mercy he can manage.

He's cycling through all this, tattooed arms perched on burning thighs, when she turns and goes. Just starts walking toward the trees, as if she's saving him the trouble of anguishing over it. There's purpose in her walk as she strides away in Abby's plaid Wellingtons and Barbie parka. A certain grace. He supposes she understands that she might as well get comfortable. Kyle watches and listens, half expecting the girl to dissolve into the evening mist before his eyes.

At the edge of the trees, though, she stops. For a second Kyle wonders if he's got it wrong—if she'll turn around and run back at him and make him say it out loud, needing to understand his tone even if she doesn't know the English words: *I'm leaving you here.*

Instead, she pulls off the parka and lets it fall down around her ankles in a marshmallowy pink heap. He's about to protest, when he sees it: the striped, bushy tail hanging from the base of her spine, protruding just above the hem of her track pants. For a distended second, it wavers like a lazy pendulum—then, answering his disbelief, twitches, a quick flick, as if to cast a spell. Soo-bin turns and gives him a curious look, black eyes rimmed with coal-dark smudge. Kyle opens his mouth to speak—say, *What are you?* Say, *I used to be better*—but before he can utter a word, she's darted off into the trees, the crackle of broken twigs prickling his ears, the grey spirit of a split moon hovering over the treeline.

Kyle squats there on the wet, rotting leaves, taking in the dense weave of branches from behind a blur of tears. With the ghost of Krista's voice murmuring in his ear something soft, something about Andy Dufresne and the warm place, he hauls himself up to get back into the truck and crank some hardcore as loud as it will go—loud enough to blot out the cracking in her voice, the wheeze of her dying breath, the flick of the cargo girl's tail, and whatever other echoes haven't fled him yet, even though he knows the music will never work that way again.

Home Range

Little Flags

Little
Flags

"**I** believe this is where the battle for civilization is being fought. I really do."

Earl Sampson ambled along the border, thumbs jammed into his belt, fingers crabbed around a huge brass belt-buckle shaped like a San Antonio rose. Two newsmen from the *Daily Star* followed him, one crouched behind a camera, the other, the reporter, poking a long microphone toward Earl's face. Earl had pushed real hard to get these clowns out to do a Fourth of July story on his new Border Hawk drones. He'd given them the complete sales pitch: design based on a golden eagle. Lightweight carbon-fibre wing structure. Only model that won't frighten local birds. It wasn't until one of the drones had actually helped nab a wetback that they'd finally bit. Earl wasn't about to waste the opportunity. He paused and flashed his best public smile, the one Helen had always said shone like the grille of an oncoming truck.

"Right here, along this border. Sure, we can build a wall—build the biggest wall you ever seen! And we're doin' it! Mile by mile, we're building it. Just like we designed, engineered, and put to the sky these state-of-the-art UAVs. I mean, take the fella they caught out in Las Cienegas just yesterday. Our Border Hawks spotted his heat signature from thirty-two thousand feet, just shy of three miles from the point of apprehension. Lord Almighty! Lopez, he said his name was. Well, they're all Lopez, aren't they?

"But my point is, you really want to fix the border problem? What you need is *vigilance*. Vigilance and will! And it ain't me I'm talking about, neither. My sunset's not so far off. What I'm doing is trying to ignite the spark of nationhood in the hearts of the *youth*."

On cue, Earl drew from his back pocket a miniature flag, black plastic wand glued with a nylon flap dyed with the stars and stripes, white cardboard label etched with tiny lines of text dangling from a string tied to its blunted spike. From the sidelines, one of his deputies, Ollie, spied the flag and leaned down to whisper to a wee pigtailed girl at his side, who skipped over to Earl and looked up at him with eyes as wide as a Colorado sky. As though conferring a blessing, Earl pressed the toy flag into the little girl's palm, squeezing her fingers around its holiness.

"This is my kind of nation-building, see? With each flag I pass on to kids like this little peach right here" — Earl patted the girl on the head — "maybe it helps 'em know what it means to be an American. What God-given rights they have, and why we can't let the illegals take those rights away from them. Not to mention the jobs! Mark my words, this country is being invaded."

He swung his arm in a wide arc across the scrubland that lay beyond the razor wire, the desert rolling down to the stricken cartel strongholds below the Rio Grande that disgorged the desperate and ambitious in equal measure toward Earl's watchful eye.

"*La Reconquista*. It's on the way. Bolivar, Pancho Villa... that revolutionary spirit is bleedin' up through the border like a coming flood."

He turned his face and stared straight into the camera, smile cranked up to chrome-plated eighteen-wheeler, pedal to the metal.

"I'm just doin' what I can to stop it."

×

Every year, leading up to the Fourth of July, the American Shield received thousands of letters of support from across the country. They poured in by mail, by email, some delivered by hand, and from each one Earl Sampson, proud founder and president of the Shield, selected a pithy excerpt, which he then had printed on a white cardboard label and tied to one of the little American flags from his stockpile, thereby imbuing cheap Chinese product with a dose of real American sentiment. He would then, in person whenever possible, place each flag in the dirt along the border fence between Cochise County and the Mexican hinterland. There were thousands of them, planted as far as you could see, a beautiful force field of red, white, and blue fluttering against the bleached landscape. On one part of the wall, near his ranch, the flags had been pinned up and arranged to spell out the words Earl Sampson held as his personal creed and mission: *SECURE THE BORDER. STOP THE INVASION.*

Earl could see the slogan from the bay window in his living room, as fine a view as any cowboy could ask for. Same as every evening, he saluted the words and the dusky sky behind them, then sank down into his leather recliner and sighed. Tonight he was extra tired from smiling for the cameras all day, and was looking forward to kicking back for the night. He liked the old westerns, *Gunsmoke* and *Rawhide* and *The Virginian*, and now with his new streaming package he could watch them all the time.

Earl shifted his gut and wiped a palm across his Stetson-greasy head as the TV glowed on, the sound of canned gunshots filling the room. It was important to be settled just right, before he called in Valentina.

In his mind, he called her his Only—as in, his Only Exception. To the boys who dared give him a look, he said the same thing every time, smiling at maximum throttle: "A girl as doggone pretty as that transcends the national interest, wouldn't you say?" In those words were contained all the ones that Earl Sampson didn't need to speak aloud: that he'd founded the Shield with money from his own god-damn pockets, and the Shield's guns were his guns, and Helen had been gone over a year now, so the wise thing was to shut the fuck up unless you wanted to spend a night discussing the matter with Earl's five German shepherds. And the boys would all nod and shrug and let it go—because you couldn't argue: Valentina was one pretty little prize. Svelte and young, with skin the colour of mocha chocolate. She'd been with him for just about six months now, shipped up from Nuevo León by a Coyote he'd got friendly with, and although she cleaned the house and prepared meals, her chief concern was to bring Earl his daily after-work glass of Pappy Van Winkle, and to otherwise help him relax and shrug off the tension born of battling the tidal wave of migrant blood that threatened to engulf his beloved country.

On the table beside him lay one of his testifying flags—*Keep Up the Good Fight! America for Americans*—and next to it, a little brass bell. Earl picked up the bell and gave a sharp ding. "Valentina, darlin'?" he shouted in singsong drawl. "It's time!"

She came at his call, resplendent in a dress of purple lace, carrying a silver tray laid with a single tumbler frosted with cold and filled with cherry-dark bourbon. Her eyes were black as opals, her frame as petite and light as a bird's. There were times when she looked mute, ignorant even; but Earl knew what kind of fight the girl had in her. She'd been a prickly cactus at first, but he'd taught her the ropes, soon enough.

"Well don't you just look adorable as all git out tonight," he said, pinching her behind. "So kind of you to bring me my little drop of medicine in such a punctual fashion." He took the glass from the tray and brought it to his lips with a satisfied slurp. "Did you see me on TV today? Then you know how tired my poor bones are. Yes, indeed, another tough day for old Earl and his brothers of the Shield."

Valentina stood still beside the chair, staring down into the silver tray held out flat in front of her. Earl looked up at her face. He liked the girl, for real. After Helen had passed, he'd found that no time patrolling the border, no amount of rifle practice, not even the affection of his beloved dogs could stop the day from coming to that hollow point of loneliness, just Earl and *Rawhide* on the TV, him getting up again and again to fill his own whiskey glass even though the bourbon wasn't any help, either. The house empty, the bougainvillea in the big pots dying because it had always been Helen who tended them. The hollow, it was nothing like Earl had ever known before. It made him feel old and strange and weak, and those weren't feelings he could tolerate, not with the mission he was on. And so he'd brought Valentina into the house on the down-low, not sure exactly what her role would be, but knowing he'd find a way to make use of her, all the same.

Earl smiled at her, not his semi-truck smile, but a gentler one. He was strong—loved being strong—but any man had times when he needed a break from the bluster. Every man needed someone to talk to, to share pleasures with. Her being Mexican...well, everyone had a tragic flaw. He'd asked the Lord for His forgiveness.

And anyway, sometimes, lying in bed at night waiting for the desert moon to sink, he wondered if he might not be doing a good thing with it. Although he would never admit it out loud, didn't even like to say it to himself, when he looked at Valentina, he knew deep down that he could never stop them. The ones crawling across the desert, they had heart—but that wasn't even it. What they had on their side, which he could never stamp out, was a longing to reach America, to taste its riches and know the real meaning of freedom. How could you talk someone out of a dream like that? How could you even blame them? They'd keep on coming, thick and hungry as a locust plague, just as long as the States kept shining its beacon out over their hardscrabble lives. Hell, half the country was already Hispanic. Although Earl would remain vigilant, would stand by his banners like a good warrior, he could see full well that the old America—the one that loved *Rawhide* and *Gunsmoke* and *The Virginian* like he did—was getting as thin as the cheap Chinese nylon on his little flags.

He hated to know it, would hate it until the day he followed Helen into the arms of the Lord, but looking up at Valentina, such a lovely dark thing, gave him a thread of solace to hold on to. The whiskey swirled round Earl's head, and he thought: *If they have to come, at least let 'em be like her.*

"Now," he said. "Let's make sure I can recuperate in time for the fireworks shows tomorrow!" He took another swig of Pappy. "I know you don't love this part as of yet, although I'm hoping you'll learn, eventually. You know I'm always telling you to trust me. You'll see it in the end—you'll thank me for everything, for giving you a place here. Even for puttin' some savings aside for you instead of letting you send it all away on that needy family of yours. Yes: remain in the care of Earl Sampson, my Valentine, and perhaps one day you'll come to know the fullness of pride and pleasure that America at its best can truly bring."

Earl heaved back and kicked up the recliner to emphasize the point.

"Maybe having watched that fella on the TV yesterday, the one we picked off a mile or so from Route 82, will drive home just how lucky you are to've landed here. It ain't nice to say it, but you know as well as I do that you could've ended up out there in the desert, feedin' the buzzards." He eased his polyester-panted legs a touch further apart and chuckled. "You know I consider you a special case. I'd hate to think of you back out there, staggering around in the dust and dark."

Without a sound, Valentina placed the tray down on the side table and came to stand in front of Earl.

"That's it. And mind, no mischief, now," he said. It was the thing Helen had always said to him before he headed out for border patrol. He'd learned it in Spanish for Valentina.

"*Ninguna travesura.* Old Earl's had a hard day."

Only she could comfort him. When a terrible fever came over him and he'd lain drained and sweating for days in the shadowed adobe room, their mother had quailed and wept and prayed to God for his recovery. But it was Valentina who'd stayed by his side, stroking his damp hair away from his eyes, whispering stories about the promised land to soothe him to sleep.

Javier wished, for a hundredth time, that she were with him now. The blue desert stretched out behind him, miles of brittle mesquite and cracked skulls and chittering rattlesnakes; but nothing was more terrifying than the crest of pink on the horizon, the blush of day. Nighttime was shadowed and tense, but the days were a crazed scramble through unbearable heat and light, easy pickings for *La Migra*'s patrolmen and the assault rifles they aimed from the backs of their armored pickups.

His vision blurred with the delirium of sleeplessness. The air was already thickening with encroaching heat. If she was here, she could put her hand on his forehead to cool it with her touch. Say, *Javi, you're almost there.*

It was over a year ago that his sister had left Monterrey to go north in search of work. For a while, she'd sent money back, three hundred American dollars a month, transferred through Western Union. Then, without warning, it had stopped. His family waited, hoping to hear word, hoping the money would start coming again. But nothing came.

Javier, the closest to her in age, insisted on going after her.

"How will you find her?" his mother said. "She could be anywhere. She could be in Canada by now. She could be dead." She wept, cursing the Americans and their money, cursing Mexico for needing it.

Javier knew his sister wasn't dead. They shared an interior language forged in those long nights when she stayed by his bedside, when they dreamed together of other places, magical futures. He could feel her whispering somewhere up past the Rio Grande. "Don't worry, Mama," he said. "I know she's alive. I'll find her." What he left out was the darkness he could feel, the sense that his sister was somehow being choked, that she was alive but death was close to her. *Valentina*, he thought. *What sickness has you?*

The sun rose into a sky striped with clouds like long clawmarks. Javier slouched down behind an outcropping of cactus and orange stone, taking what rest he could before the morning was fully upon him. He looked out to the distance. He'd been walking for three days. Yesterday's supper had used up his last bits of food. He had only a half bottle of water left, which he brought to his mouth for a few sparing sips. He had to be close: there was no other way to think.

He stood and began his slow, shuffling walk once more. The sun's heat sneered over the hills, already beginning to bake his chapped lips. He kept stumbling, trying not to fall, to add more bruises and scrapes to the ones purpled and weeping on his elbows and knees. Above him, a buzzard circled the sky, watching. He lurched forward and threw his arms up into the air and croaked. The bird flew off northward, crossing borders without concern.

Hours passed and the sun reached its blistering apex. He tried to keep an image of his sister in his mind — to hold on to the picture of her leaning over him, her blue dress washed with gold in the lamplight, administering him sips of chilled, sweet hibiscus tea. To call her forth from that place and that time in which she'd fit so perfectly. But the image blurred in the heat, her face turning to gnarled tumbleweeds, her dark eyes spiked through with the flitting tongues of red, white, and blue snakes.

Javier closed his eyes and craned his face skyward. The sun made the inside of his lids glow the colour of rust. When he opened them, the buzzard had come back. There was another one with it. They circled and dipped toward him, something in their turning making him look closer. There was no patience in their curves; their hunger was harder, more insistent.

When he heard the whine of their motors he knew. Not buzzards, but crafts with no pilots, bodies with no hearts. Pure, merciless vision.

Drones.

Fear and adrenalin flooded his muscles and threw him into a run. Blind running, running anywhere, in search of cover that didn't exist in this wide-open hell, running with whatever energy he had left in the direction he believed might lead him to safety. To his sister, still alive up there, stalked by darkness. The dust and grit and heat poured into him, and he began coughing, little catches to start, then huge, wracking coughs, his whole trunk convulsing and threatening to split apart and spill his organs out onto the baking earth. The power in his legs dissolved, giving way under the weight of his hurtling body, pitching him forward into the scrub. His cheekbone met the dirt and his vision went black.

Amid the high ringing and the warm touch of blood he fixed her in his mind and his chest, fused his own pounding heartbeats to hers, so that each would know exactly when the other's stopped beating. He opened his shredded mouth and although he made no sound, called to her.

Valentina.

By the time he looked up and saw the green-and-white pickup truck bouncing over the horizon, dozens of little American flags lining its hood, he had to call it a victory. He would not die in the desert. They would send him back, but he'd be alive. To wait for her, again. Or the next chance to go after her.

Two men in fatigues jumped down from the truck and hauled him up by the arms, holding him out like a trophy deer for the cameraman that followed them. Another man, this one wearing a big suede Stetson and orange sunglasses and an embroidered cowboy shirt bulging with his gut, waddled over and stood in front of him, fingers hooked into a huge rose-shaped belt buckle.

"What's your name, son?" he said.

Javier hung like a scarecrow. Sunlight blazed into his face and he squinted and groaned at the pain in his head, like a metal cog grinding away at the bone under his eye. Her face swelled up in his mind, and then folded into ripples and collapsed, like a stilled flag.

"Lopez," he said. "Javier Lopez."

✕

Valentina kneeled in front of him, rubbing, squeezing. There were veins and callouses and hard edges, his feet pale and misshapen from years stuffed into hot boots treading rocky ground. The last two toes on each foot were clubbed, the nails yellowed and thick. She heard him take another long, oily swallow of bourbon and sigh. Some TV western blared out behind her, all tinny orchestra music and buckaroo drawl. Valentina closed her eyes and kneaded his troll's feet, reciting out, with each application of pressure, a mantra in her mind. *Last time. Last time. Last time.*

She rubbed and pressed patiently, until the first twitch came, quick and sharp. Then another, a longer convulsion. She paused, holding his limp feet in her hands like a hunk of moist cheese, and now he wrenched and turned and pitched his glass to roll across the floor, emptied of the strong and fragrant bourbon, the extra squeeze of Nayarit coral snake venom she'd added in. Above her, his face reddened and swelled like a morning sun, suffused with his proud blood. As he thrashed, she listened to his choking, watched streams of white foam dribble from his lips. Even in the throes of death, he was so pink and fat, so much like a greased ham.

She thought about how thin Javier had looked, her brother's smashed-in face recoiling from the cameras, golden skin whitened to ash, blue splotches darkening his eyes, making the ripped-open flesh of his left cheek all the more vivid as it streamed with blood. He was broken, defeated, and they held up his defeat like a banner, echoing the words that Earl Sampson had emblazoned on his cursed fence.

Valentina Lopez let go of the dead man's feet. She reached over and picked up the little flag on the side table, which she waved once in a feeble victory salute before sliding its cheap, wobbly stem into the pocket of Earl Sampson's cowboy shirt. The sun was nearly set, and she would need to be far away before morning came. He would be expected at the parade. When he didn't show, they would look for him. Then for her.

She grabbed the knapsack she'd stashed behind the curtain that morning, and stripped off her purple dress, quickly changing into the dark sweats she'd plucked from the closet where his dead wife's clothing still hung. When she slid open the glass door, the humid night rushed in at her, alive with the sizzle of crickets and the murmur of wind over the dirt, like a song pulling her forward into the nighttime, away from Monterrey, away from Cochise County, toward the silvered wonderland of America.

She thought about Javier, surely now slouched in the back of some filthy truck bouncing back down the rutted road to home. She thought about their crumbling house there with its suffocating adobe rooms, the time she'd watched her brother shiver through the fever for nine days, almost dying in the dust and heat. She remembered the stories she'd told him, about the land of hopes and dreams.

She was the one who'd made it. She was across now.

Above her, the stars were coming out, mirroring the twinkle of Tucson's lights visible to the northwest, below the dark ridge of the Santa Catalina Mountains. She wanted to know it, all of it... *the fullness of pride and pleasure.* Behind her, a huge spangled flag stirred atop the late Earl Sampson's ranch, gesturing toward the horizon, whispering its promise.

Sheepasnörus Rex

SSSHH*HHHHHHHHHHHHHHHHHHHHHHHHHHHHHHH*
HHHHHHHHHHHHHHHHHHHHHHHHHHHHHHHHHHH
HHHHHHHHHHHHHHHHHHHHHHHHHHHHHHHHHHHH
HHHHHHHHHHHHHHHHHHHHHHHHHHHHHHHHHHHHH
HHHHHHHHHHHHHHHHHHHHHHHHHHHHHHHHHHHHP

Quiet fell on the room like a cleaver. Where before a soothing hush had percolated from the countertop monitor, like a warm towel draped so comfortably over the atmosphere that Craig had stopped noticing it, now there was only gaping, cosmic silence — and only one way to fill it, one possible outcome.

When the sheep stopped, the screaming began.

On cue, the monitor crackled to life with the sound of Rosie's shrieks. She'd only been down for twenty-five minutes. Not enough, not enough. Now she'd need a change and a bottle and most of all, her mom, who was probably still in the middle of the liturgy or creed or some other weird part of a ritual they'd both agreed was ridiculous until Elise got pregnant and discovered her lapsed Catholic faith growing in tandem with the baby. Craig stood by the kitchen counter, staring at a nugget of oatmeal congealed on the lip of a pot stacked in the sink, and fought down the questions burping up into his chest. *Are you so terrified of her waking up? So rattled by an infant? Dad?*

In theory, his weekly solo parenting sessions were easy. His duties consisted primarily of maintaining the conditions for Rosette to nap. But the sheep was critical to this. When it failed, it triggered a whole chain of incompetence: Craig fumbling through a diaper change, then trying to push a bottle of defrosted breast milk into

Rosie's wailing mouth as he carted her back and forth between the living room and kitchen, singing soft nonsense in a ridiculous voice, dribbling milk all over the floor, his nerves chafed raw as tuna sashimi.

In truth, it ate at him that he needed a piece of cheap, mass-produced crap to preserve his sanity whenever he was alone with the baby. That on Sunday mornings, tension clung to him like a sour, flatulent funk as he surrendered control to a ridiculous doodad somehow possessed of both the witchcraft necessary to get Rosette to stay asleep and a functional inconsistency that bordered on sadism.

For this dark magic—the tuneless, mercurial song that brought calm to his child when he could not—Craig had come to loathe the bastard, Sheepasnörus.

✕

"The fucking sheep has *no clutch*! No. Clutch. At. All!"

He whapped the sheep's soft plush head against the lip of the vintage Formica table. On the chair beside him, Rosette cooed in her bassinet. Elise stood by the counter in a grey skirt and floral church blouse, squeezing tubes of Cha-Zee-Zee spread and Bruschetta Blend onto pieces of toast. In the fluorescence, her skin was almost translucent.

"It's supposed to shut off after a certain amount of time," she said. "It assumes she's asleep."

"And what if she *needs* it to sleep? What then? Then it's a piece of shit with *no clutch*."

"Language," said Elise.

"What, is God listening?"

She frowned at him. "I'm listening. And Rosette is. That's not enough?"

It wasn't a sheep, exactly. Sheepasnörus was half lamb, half dinosaur, two silver vinyl horns, googly eyes, and a floppy spinal ridge sewn onto a snuggly bag of cotton batting housing a battery casing and the speaker box that produced its four varieties of soothing white noise. In the logo on its tag, the umlaut over the *o* was rendered as little cartoon lamby ears. Craig couldn't say if Rosette loved its whooshing or not—wasn't sure when she'd start being able to love things. Regardless, her being unable to sleep without it was untenable; it was madness, to rely on something so unreliable.

Craig's stomach gurgled. He took a mouthful of coffee, heavily spiked with Bailey's. Elise chewed toast slathered with the gloppy, sodium-rich condiments their house had been lousy with ever since Elise's uncle had caved and agreed to give Craig a shot at junior marketing executive at KBC-Flaxos. She paused the argument to beam at Rosette and brush a strand of oily hair away from the baby's face. Craig looked at his tiny daughter, her pale feather-fuzz over skin as soft as butter. For an instant, she caught his look with her wide, searching eyes, and he felt his heart lurch under his ribs.

God, he loved her. Both of them, both of them. Wrenching, desperate love.

He was so tired.

Elise was more tired. She unbuttoned her blouse for a feeding, a faint pink glow coming into her cheeks as she looked at Rosette. Sunlight from the window made a halo around her wispy hair. Mothering drained and recharged her. It was all beautiful to watch, hard to live through. Small things got inflamed, out of control before you knew it. The sheep, for instance: it was feeding off their weakness, an evil larva suckling on their fatigue, engorging itself. It had to go.

"I'm taking it out to the shed," he said, shaking Sheepasnörus so that its googly eyes tittered and spun, clicking like moths trapped under glass. "Maybe I can fix it so that it doesn't shut off. Tinker with it."

Elise raised an eyebrow at him, a smear of Cha-Zee-Zee on her lip. "It's not your Sheepasnörus," she said, scooping up the baby. Rosette crossed her eyes and farted a loud squelch, an astonishing sound from a body so small. Elise scrunched up her nose and grinned. "Do we need to be changed?"

"I'm taking it out to the shed," said Craig.

✕

That night Rosette wailed for a full hour before falling asleep. Elise kept giving Craig stern looks, but on this he wouldn't budge: the sheep was staying outside. After a marathon of hoarse lullabies, he agreed to a compromise and called up a white-noise app on his phone, and the baby finally fell into an exhausted calm.

Afterwards, they sat, frazzled and limp over bowls of turkey chili. Craig drank beer and Elise had lemonade, and they watched *Mad Men* on TV until ten thirty, when their eyes began to droop and the foot massage Craig was giving Elise dwindled to a feeble pinching of her big toe. They went quietly up to bed, Craig hyper-aware of every creaky step or popping of his ankle. Tired as he was, a good rest was still months away; tonight there'd be a three a.m. feed and another in early morning, before seven. When they got into bed, he picked up the thick paperback copy of Stephen King's *It* that he'd been reading for the past four months, stared at the page for ten minutes, then fell asleep with the book on his chest.

Sometime later, he woke to a twinge in his bladder. He resisted opening his eyes to look at the clock. The air smelled of old sweat. Dust tickled his throat. He thought about that afternoon, about Sheepasnörus out in the shed, condemned to slump on the cluttered workbench amid pine shavings and cobwebs and rusty screws. In the moment, it seemed absurd, to have exiled an inanimate stuffy that was helping them through this lunacy. Something churned in his gut, and he felt a belch push up into his esophagus. He sat up to let it out, and the book tumbled from his chest onto the floor, with a thump that made him wince. He reached to get it, and when he rose again, the monster was there, in front of him.

It perched at the foot of the bed, huge and damp, breathing in heavy rasps, its wide black eyes glossy and indifferent. Milky goo streamed from its sluglike lips and dripped down a belly as broad and pale as boiled haggis. Its curled horns were calcified into scaly bone, and it had a tufted Satan-beard of cornsilk hair under its blunt nose. A pair of hooves jutted from its torso, wavering as though unmoored from the consciousness of its body, as it swayed ever so slightly back and forth on rumpled haunches of pink skin.

Its presence keened through Craig's body like antifreeze. His mind screamed, *What the fuck what the fuck?*—even though he knew. There was no way it could be real, this gross, corpulent hallucination of his daughter's mechanical sleep aid, sheep-aid, snorasaur, piece of junk, plastic god. This was exhaustion, or his Ativan mixed with one too many Budweisers.

"Hello, Carl," it said.

Craig felt a reaching in his diaphragm, an upchuck of words: "My name's C-Craig."

"It doesn't matter," said Sheepasnörus. Its voice issued from somewhere near its groin, calm and deep, layered and laced with a tapelike hiss. Craig looked at Elise. She was asleep, her face round and peaceful. She couldn't hear the ghost.

I'm also a ghost, Craig thought.

The thing wheezed, weeping fluid.

"I'm in the garage, Carl. I can't soothe in distance*shhhh.*"

Was it revenge? An omen? Had he been drugged? Brainwashed? Could he possibly be tired enough that he was hallucinating? He resisted the urge to talk back to the thing.

"You're tired...I can help you*ssshhh.*"

"I don't want your help," Craig said, by reflex. It was all fine, fine.

"You know Rosette can't sleep without me," said Sheepasnörus.

"She's sleeping now."

"It won't last, Carl." It paused, oozing. "I have the soul of your child."

"*NO!* No!" Craig almost shouted, loud enough to wake the baby. He put a hand to his mouth, bit down on his index finger. "I can also provide for you*sssschhhhh*," said Sheepasnörus. Its black tongue flashed out, curling into a swizzle. "Your friends are all richer than you. You'll never play soccer. I know about the Whopper lunches, Carl. Accept it: *you're not really here.* Leave your body behind. I'll make sure it continues caring for the woman and child. For your soul, there is a better pla*schhhhhhe*."

Craig's mind reeled, conjuring hilly roads, ocean vistas, mountaintop palaces; a white beach house in San Diego, piña colada glasses frosted with condensation; palm leaves, lightness, distance. Himself, strong but without weight.

Then the smell of Rosette's hair hit him, warm and sweet and cookie-like, and he felt something being pulled from within his body, like a knot of chewed food dragged up through his intestine. Sheepasnörus drew its steaming, muttony snout close to his face and lashed its tongue across his pajama-clad chest, probing.

"We're famished, Carl. *Famished forever.*"

"This isn't happening!"

"The bounty of youth has past." Sheepasnörus sat back, licking its chops. "*Now is the time of sacrificeshhhhhhhhhh!*" Hooves flailing, it arched its snout skyward, revealing a patchy wattle of veins, and began a mad, desperate panting, punctuated with cracked bleats, which quickly rose into a sound like a chainsaw ripping through bark, splintering Craig's skull.

×

In the morning, he remembered coming to in front of the open fridge, staring into its humming depths at shelves full of half-wrapped cheeses and jalapeño jellies, clutching a leftover meatball sub like a burning torch, unsure of how he'd gotten downstairs but aware of a pressure in his temples that was unfamiliar to him. Elise came and met him on his way back to the bedroom, saying, *Are you all right? I saw you weren't in bed.* Her face blue in the shadows, a holy thing.

×

"It's a big change. Big, oh yeah."

Stephen sat, leaning on a bottle of Budweiser, nodding his head and staring at the TV above the bar, where Lionel Messi was helping Barça take apart Villarreal. Craig had known Stephen for seventeen years, since he'd come over from Mauritius to go to university and they'd shared a dorm room. Now his friend had a three-year-old son and made wheelbarrows of money writing security code for a software company. They saw each other every two or three months, a bit more often since Elise got pregnant. Stephen was the no-brainer to call after Craig had begged for an afternoon out of the house, craving beer; he and his wife, Gwen, were trying out a separation, sharing their kid, Dexter, on alternating weeks. Stephen knew all about escape.

"I'm just overtired," Craig said. He hoped it was true. He'd come to the bar desperate to unload about the Sheepasnörus nightmare. But amid the clinking glassware and fuzzy Springsteen tune pumping from the speakers, he wasn't sure he was ready to sound quite so insane.

Their bartender came over, a thin, slouchy girl who smelled like Juicy Fruit.

"Another?" she said.

"Two," said Craig. "For us. One each for him and me." He waggled a finger between him and Stephen, who had barely made a dent in his first drink. He followed his friend's eyes up to the TV. Messi was weaving his way through a glut of players like a homing bee.

"There's this noise machine Rosette has," Craig said, tentative, voice quivering. "It's been driving me up the wall."

"Unh-huh. The toys'll get you. For a while Gwen wouldn't allow Dexter anything with batteries. It was great. Didn't last."

The waitress brought two fresh bottles.

"I guess it's more than just being tired," said Craig, wondering how deeply he could trust Stephen to field his neuroses. Whether he could talk to his friend about how time had become warped since Rosette was born. How she had forced him into a new shape, one he wasn't sure he could maintain. "I guess I'm feeling a bit helpless. Invisible."

Stephen turned to him. He held out his bottle for a cheers. Craig picked up his Budweiser and clinked it.

"Fuck it," said Stephen. "You ain't never gonna be Lionel Messi, but I like hanging out with you."

Craig smiled, but the statement rattled him. The calm, hissing voice came back: *You'll never play soccer.* It had known him. All the ways in which he'd failed, all his anxieties, all the dreams he hated for not going away.

"This stuff never bothers Elise the same way," Craig said. "She's always so . . . *present* with Rosie. Her attention, her patience, it never falters, you know? How does she do it, Steve?"

On TV, Messi scored again. Stephen took a sip of Bud. "Two things," he said. "Number one, women, they just have this thing. An instinct. We'll never be mothers; just dads. Different role. Moms carry most of the emotional weight of the first year."

"What's two?"

"Two is, she has to do it, because you don't."

"I will!" said Craig. "I'm willing." He would do anything for Rosette, anything.

"Sorry, wrong word," said Stephen. "You *can't.*"

On the stereo, Springsteen moaned that he was tired and bored of himself. When Craig was little, his parents had played this record on vinyl and danced around the living room to it, singing into candlesticks. Decades later, here it was: the same damn song. He dragged the bottom of his beer over the mosaic bar top, bits of coloured glass embedded in white plaster. It made a hollow clunking. The Boss, Messi: they thrilled millions. This was what Craig contributed—empty music of a half-drunk beer in the musty afternoon light of a city pub, soundtrack to an emergency meeting he'd called to confess his dealings with a monstrous, sedative sheep.

He felt tears welling up and swallowed them. He was tired, not weak like some old man, some sad condiment salesman terrified of being alone with his daughter for longer than half the length of a soccer match. Rosette would love him. She had to.

"Do you ever think about your kid watching you die?" he said.

Stephen gave Craig a flat look. He put down his beer. "My Uncle Anil," he said. "He had three kids, my cousins. Two weeks before the family was supposed to leave Mauritius, he went for a walk down to the rum shop and keeled over on the way. Cardiac arrest; dead in minutes. No one there with him. His kids were at home, watching *The Price Is Right*. My kid, your kid: who knows where they'll be when we go. It's all a gamble, man. No one knows shit."

He raised another cheers, drained his beer and grabbed the new one. "We'll finish these," he said. "Then you need to go home to your girls."

Time ran down and Barça took the game. Messi strolled off the field, nonchalant in victory, a true champion. Craig stared into the glow of the liquor stocks over the bar, looking for Elise's face, for Rosette's, watching dust drift through the neon lights and settle on the bottletops.

×

He got home four beers later, slouched but calmed, the tension in his muscles loosened enough that he could admire the blush in the sky, the warmth in the breeze. Stephen had been easy to coax into a few more. Craig had texted Elise to make sure she was okay to get Rosette down alone, promised to make her dinner the next day, give her an extra-long foot rub before bed.

The lights in the living room were on, but instead of going in he went around the back and into the yard. The door to the shed was closed but not locked, and he opened it slowly, to prevent it from creaking. The bare bulb threw a thin white gloss over the workbench. Sheepasnörus leaned against the slats of damp grey wood, paw resting on a rusty old vise grip that Craig never used. He stood in front of the cursed toy, looking down at it, feeling his pulse piston in his neck. What now. What now. What now.

A whiff of gasoline blew in on the wind as the thing twitched, stood up on its stubby snack-cake legs, took two steps forward as though preparing to bow, and spoke — the force of it, the terrible ordinariness, making Craig reel backward into a stand of old rakes: "I lied before, you know," it said. Its voice was smaller now, more muffled, but still carried its undercurrent of sibilance, the undulance of breath.

Craig caught his balance. He was awake. Wide awake; there was no mistaking this. He felt an itch behind his ear, a crick in his knee. He gaped at the thing, sweat pouring down his back.

"When?" he said. "About what?"

"You can play soccer. I can give you his place."

"Who?"

"Messi*shhh*." Sheepasnörus gave a little hop-skip and a kick, miming the Argentine's dribbling. "He owes us a debt."

"Us?"

"Me and you, Carl."

Craig squeezed his eyes shut. He was losing it. There was no way out of this. The thing would not leave him, not admit the impossibility of its presence.

"Nuh," he said. A blunt negation, all he could manage.

"You want to play? Don't you? Be best*sssshhh*?"

Sheepasnörus Rex

"Yes! No! Why?"

"Lionel Messi is a very rich man."

Craig grabbed a rake from the stash and held it in front of him like a wizard's staff, hands around the wooden pole, eyes peering through the fan of bent red metal. He considered the grain on the handle, the parts where different hands had worn it smooth. It had been Elise's grandfather's rake. It had years on it. Smashing it on the workbench would surely snap the teeth off.

"You're lying," Craig said. "You can't."

"I know you're considering it."

Craig winced. He wasn't; he was. In his mind, in his chest, he could feel the racing of Lionel Messi's feet across the pitch, fluttering with energy, graceful and precise, always knowing what to do. How to be such a man? To fly, to move fluidly through the morass of the world: you had to give something up.

"Yes, just like that. It's easy. Take my hand." Sheepasnörus held out a nubbly plush paw. Outside, a breeze made the maples hiss. A cat meowed. Something in the bowels of the shed began ticking. Craig tasted metal on the back of his tongue, felt the smoothed wood on his palm, Messi's nimble footwork in his stomach and his shaking calves, felt a heat in his neck, pressure on his teeth, the floor collapsing below him.

With a whipped flick, he threw the rake aside and reached out to grab Sheepasnörus, one fist curling around the offered paw, the other gripping the plush folds of its opposite thigh. He hoisted the haunted gizmo into the air in front of him, so it was framed by the dusty window, where a million tiny flies had alighted and died on the sill.

"Ye*sshhhhhh*," said Sheepasnörus. Soothing, somnolent. "Ye*sshhhhhhhhhh . . .*"

Screeching like a crazed, wounded hawk, Craig pushed all the strength he could into his toxified blood and reefed on the sheep's arm, twisting and pulling until he felt the snarling resistance of the threads, and pulled harder, until the arm went *whuff* and split off from the torso, leaving a spill of cotton batting spooling out into the electrified air between host and limb. He flailed, wailed, shook the sheep, flopped it around on the workbench like a mess of dough. The hissing got louder, rent by bursts of radio crackle. Craig snatched a ball-peen hammer from the wall rack, took aim, and brought it down on the speaker box, crushing through plastic and wires, stuffing and tiny screws.

When he realized he was yelling his own name, over and over and over, he stopped. Let the silence of the shed infuse him.

But now there was another sound—round, wet, percussive, like a steady rhythm played on a miniature sealskin drum. Craig knew it. Its fragility, its surprise. He'd heard it before, channelled by a gelled wand through a speaker; felt it bumping gently through muscle and skin to vibrate in a hand placed on Elise's stomach, searching for the unknown child inside.

Craig squinted at the dismembered arm in his right hand. He tossed it on the bench in disgust. Crouching, breathing hard, he peered into the cavity on Sheepasnörus' chest. There, nestled among the cotton, sat a tiny delicate heart, gemlike and robed in jellied red, beating out the code of life: *whumsh, whumsh, whumsh, whumsh, whumsh, whumsh*...

He reached out a finger, touched the living flesh. Somehow him, but not.

⨯

Back inside, the air was humid and perfumed with the rubbery, powdered smell of diapers. Elise was already upstairs. Craig stopped in the kitchen before going up and poured himself a drink of water from the tap. He stood and felt the cold, mineral liquid course down his trunk.

At the top of the stairs, he paused at the master bedroom, keeping his hands with their clumsily doctored burden behind him. The room glowed with the warm light of the bedside lamp. Elise lay atop the covers, eyes closed, a copy of *The Happiest Baby on the Block* splayed on the table beside her.

"Hey," she said, without opening her eyes. "Can you try and be quiet when you go to the bathroom? She's asleep."

He took a moment to look at Elise—his wife. Rosette's mom. The lamplight on her resting face revealed the soft shape of youth coming through the lingering weariness of daytime. He thought back to when they'd met, on a patio with ivy-covered walls, trading smiles under strands of lights. At all the years since, those chapters of love and faith, the entangling and partitioning of minds, the closeness of skin —all leading up to that night in the hospital, when they'd pulled Rosette from inside her, white and squawking in terror of life. The film of sweat on his wife's face afterward. How she whispered to him the question they'd sat with for nine months: *What is it?*

Craig turned and walked, slowly, down the shadowed hall to Rosette's room. The door was open a crack. He pushed on it and went in. His daughter was a tiny cocoon in the darkness, rising and falling with uneven breaths, some catching and shuddering out in frightened sighs. A patch of dark hair swirled on her forehead, fine as eddying black sand. The soft folds under her eyes mirrored Craig's own.

The fact of her, the strange newness—it shook him, destabilized him like nerve gas, like a blinding kiss. She was everything. All of him, all his dreams...and he *wanted* that. For her to be *next*. To know all the love and wonder it was possible to know. To never feel rage, or sorrow, or hurt; to exist forever in fragile simplicity. To never feel disappointed in herself, even though she would. To know she could never disappoint him. Even though she would.

He stood beside her and cradled Sheepasnörus in his hands, its torn arm reattached with a wrapping of silver duct tape, bits of sawdust and flaked plastic clinging to its matted fur. Heart climbing into his throat, he flipped the switch on its back, summoning a low hushing noise, dull and crackly but still audible, a fractured sound to match her breathing. He placed it in the corner of his daughter's crib, close to the tiny shell of her ear. "I'm sorry," he whispered, tears blurring the darkness. "I'm sorry."

Pavilion

As the time approached for me to come face to face with the Golden Temple, which I had never yet seen, a certain hesitation grew within me.

—Yukio Mishima, *The Temple of the Golden Pavilion*

Listen, faced with the living cockroach, the worst discovery was that the world is not human, and that we are not human.

—Clarice Lispector, *The Passion According to G.H.*

i. Two houses stand at opposite ends of my public life. The first is the house that I owned. It was a white clapboard Victorian on Gore Street, just east of City Park, close to the lake. When we moved in after I was elected to city council, it was still a fixer-upper, full of dust and mould and peeling paint.

And roaches, of course — the roaches have always been with me.

It took months, but I cleaned the place up. Got it feeling like a real home, the kind of big old house you see in the movies, where happy families live. There's a photograph from that time, taken for an early profile in the *Whig-Standard*, when I was still a fresh face on council. In it, the three of us are standing on the front steps: me in the middle with Sandra and Eleanor on either side of me. We're all dressed in bright summer colours, and the photo is shot from below and framed so that a halo of sunlight rings the Canada flag hung from the gable over the front door.

That's the image I try and hold on to now, when I'm reminded where I've ended up — in this apartment that smells of old grease and ammonia and the piss-covered toilet that runs all day long, where everything is yellow and dim and I'm alone with the fragments of myself that are left.

The roaches are here, too. Skittering across the linoleum, or poking, half-visible, from underneath the fridge or the bed or the dresser. Infantry for the host, tiny emissaries of the greater pestilence that lies, engorged, under the foundation of that other house, the one at the end — the house that owned me, for a time.

They're a constant presence, the roaches. Except when I'm cleaning the rifle. When the scent of steel and ethanol fills the air, the purity of true conviction — then, the vermin run.

A house is a place for living in. But it's been a long time since anything human lived in Bellevue House.

The original was built in 1840, by Charles Hales, a merchant of the early Kingston rich. It was one of the first examples of the Italian Villa style in Canada, an imposing, L-shaped building with white stucco walls and terracotta roofs and trim painted dark hunter green. But the reason it lasted has nothing to do with its architecture. Bellevue House is revered because of its association with Sir John A. Macdonald.

Kingston is a town that's proud of its history, and few men cast a longer shadow over it than the country's first prime minister. Macdonald lived in Bellevue House for a year, between 1848 and 1849. It was supposed to be a country retreat to help his wife, Isabella, recover from illness. A refuge from the stresses of public life, bathed in the tonic air of Lake Ontario. Before a year had passed, though, Bellevue House took its first victim. The Macdonalds' firstborn son, John Alexander Jr., died at thirteen months old. Isabella got worse, tuberculosis festering in her lungs like a nest of termites.

Death has lived at Bellevue House since the very beginning. I should have known it would come for my family, in time.

2. There are so many versions of the story now, it's hard to hold on to the real one. That's the idea, of course. The more you refract the truth, the more doubt you sow in people's minds, the easier it is to lull them into a nightmare they don't even know is happening. No one is immune. I wasn't.

These days, the version most people know is from the hit movie.

I've watched the whole thing hundreds of times. All 166 minutes of it. There are two scenes I always go back to, though, key moments designed to move the narrative subtly but purposefully away from the facts. Both take place in the mayor's office. The first comes early in the film, and it's the perfect set-up for the hatchet job to come.

Mayor Jim Staughton, Councilman Tyson Webb, and Councilman Tim Gant are standing around a big oak desk laid with three glasses and a decanter of whiskey. Robert Downey Jr. plays the mayor. DiCaprio's Webb. Tim Gant is played by some pale, mousy no-name, a B-list Steve Buscemi lookalike that you can't help but loathe from the start.

"Gentlemen," the mayor says. "Let's talk about Bellevue House."

"Sir," says Gant, snivelling, "we've started charting out how to tackle it from a risk-assessment perspective—"

"That business-school methodology garbage won't cut it with this one, Gant," says the mayor, scowling. "This story's got the potential to go absolutely nuclear. We already have people on social media calling Macdonald a butcher. Granted, that's what makes the whole plan possible in the first place. But the bigger it gets, the bigger the potential shitstorm. We had the *Globe and Mail* calling the office this morning for comment. We're juggling political plutonium here. So let's get out the big guns and make sure we turn this crisis into an opportunity, shall we?"

Gant tugs at his collar. "With the right team—"

"No team!" says the mayor/Downey Jr., channelling his best Tony Stark. "This *is* the fucking team. I won't jeopardize this project by handing it over to a bunch of numb-nut staffers. Zocalar is trusting us on this. It's an unprecedented opportunity to replace a tired old heritage property with something bold, innovative. Jobs, culture, tourism—they don't make legacy projects any juicier than this. The three of us, leaving our goddamn mark on the city! But if we louse it up, it's a fucking bloodbath. Entrails, heads on spikes, the whole bit. Understand?"

To this point in the scene, Tyson Webb—the youngest of the three—has been silent, wearing a classic DiCaprio smirk, just right for a character being set up as a rakish hero. Now he leans forward in his chair and touches the table, fingers splayed to create little fortresses with his hands, skinny tie dangling between them like a black tongue. There's a long pause, which slowly fills with the hiss of backwards cymbals on the soundtrack.

"Gentlemen," he says. "It's game time. The arena is packed. I'd hate to see two of the best political minds in the history of Kingston lose their *fortitude* before the opening buzzer. Remember: we have this covered."

Hard cut to Staughton and Gant looking at each other, eyebrows raised. "*Do* we have it covered?" the mayor asks. "Do we absolutely? Do we truly understand how combustible this situation is? Tyson? How many ways there are for us to end up tied to burning stakes? Or sunk to the bottom of the river in bags filled with concrete and lye? It has to look *organic*. Not a single fucking iota of information tying us to the protests or to Zocalar can leave this circle."

"Sir, if I may," says Gant. "I couldn't agree more, which is why we've taken all the precautions. But if we—"

"BOYS," says Webb, his voice raised in an overly theatrical way, even by Hollywood standards. There's a light on him that makes his skin shimmer and his eyes shine like glass spheres offering the viewer a glimpse of his righteous soul. "It's going to work. The players are all lined up. We just have to execute. *With conviction.* Sell it right, and the rubes won't even know what's happening in front of them."

The mayor stares at him, hard. Shakes his head.

"You'd better be goddamn right, Webb."

Tyson Webb (or DiCaprio) smiles a smile so cryptic and infuriating it would make the Mona Lisa gag. On the soundtrack, a single, deep cello note begins playing in slow staccato as the camera crawls in toward him.

"Let's not forget that this isn't just some small-change development deal," he says, seizing the monologue. "This is the big time, men. It's a matter of hearts and minds. The people will follow, if we show them the way." He uncaps the decanter and pours three big glasses of golden whiskey. "We're all going to win here. Trust me." Raising his glass, he looks back and forth between his two colleagues, daring them to challenge his air of manifest destiny.

The mayor looks out the window, gnawing at his bottom lip. This suggestion of doubt is what ultimately saves his character—the implication that some inner moral compass is forcing him to wrestle with the crimes he helped engineer, clearing the way for the true villain of the story to emerge. Credit to Downey for selling it the way he does.

"Fuck it. Your game, Webb. But if this goes bad, I'm going to cut off your prick and feed it to the press gallery in a kaiser bun. Are we clear?"

"It's covered," says Webb.

Downey/Staughton picks up his glass and waves it at B-lister/Tim Gant.

"All right then," the mayor says. "The first protest goes tomorrow at noon. Gant, you're responsible for making sure they all sign the NDAs. Nobody, I mean nobody, gets paid without that signature. Webb, I want the first news story out by two p.m. Linda at CBC is already teed up. No dropping balls on this. Are we clear?"

Tim Gant—in the film, too weak to protest, devoid of any inner struggle of his own, a peon and a pawn, pathetic human smear —nods in silence and picks up his own tumbler. The three men clink glasses and take a long drink to seal their pact, and the scene fades to black on the blaring of horns.

3. Sandra knew something was wrong from the very first day. We were washing dishes together after dinner. Cold wind off the lake rattled the windows. On the radio, the last bars of "New Orleans Is Sinking" gave way to the news. Bellevue House was the lead story.

"Indigenous protesters demonstrating outside the historic home of Sir John A. Macdonald have drawn a response from city council, as lurid new rumours have emerged about his conduct..."

I felt Sandra tense up beside me. As a rule, we tried not to talk about work. Between her professorship at the university and my position on council, our family could have too easily been swallowed by our careers. But I'd been edgier than usual, and she'd noticed.

"Is that something you're involved in?" she said, nodding at the radio. "Sounds complicated."

"Some people don't think so," I said. I considered telling her everything—about the backroom deal I'd made with Staughton and Webb; about our arrangement with the Quebec developer, Zocalar; about the plan to use old Sir John and his crimes against humanity as a tool to get the result we wanted: a revitalized waterfront and a new centre for arts and culture, built by our good friends from Montreal. This was my window, to let her in.

"I know a little bit, but it's not my file," I said.

She knew I was lying, but nodded anyway.

I placed the last bowl in the cupboard and went into the living room, where Eleanor was watching TV. Seeing my daughter was both antidote and venom: being around her, watching her grow into a beautiful little person, gave me the righteousness of parenthood to hold on to, even while I knew that what I'd done, was still doing, could hurt her if it went the wrong way.

"What are you watching?" I asked. I could see that it was *Despicable Me*, the animated film with Steve Carell as the lovable supervillain Gru.

"Movie," she said, gaze fixed on the screen.

I dropped into the easy chair beside the sofa and let out a deep sigh. Then the movie went to commercial, and my blood went sour as vinegar. The room seemed to fold in on itself as the picture appeared on screen: a dreamy, rotating drone shot of Bellevue

House, its green gables shining in the autumn sun. A voice like fresh, hard butter spoke out over the image: *"A city's heritage is its heart. It feeds our culture. Our memory. Our dreams. It keeps us alive."* This dissolved to a montage of close-ups, the camera crawling slowly up the house's walls, showing off the creamy texture of the exterior stucco, the dazzle of sunlight on the golden front steps. The voice was joined by a loud drumbeat. *"Now, corrupt bureaucrats want to rip out the city's heart..."* There was another dissolve to two flags waving against a blue sky, the standards of city and country flying side by side, and between them in the sky an image, ghostly but unmistakable, of the face of Sir John A. Macdonald himself. This faded to a wide shot of Bellevue House at night, overlaid with an icon of a bright red heart, pulsing and dripping blood in time with the beat of the drum. *"Help save the city's heart,"* said the voice. *"Help save Bellevue House."* A tiny line of text at the bottom of the screen said the ad had been paid for by the Sons of Khepri. It was the first time I saw the phrase—and it was like swallowing a rancid apple, core and all, and feeling the seeds take root inside you.

Eleanor was entranced. From the doorway, Sandra had caught the last half of the ad, too. I wondered if she noticed me turning white as a grub. I wondered how much she knew, and whether it broke her heart to watch it happen.

4. The next week, the posters appeared. Dozens were plastered to lampposts and construction barriers in the downtown core, and two billboards went up in Confederation Basin, all bearing the same image: Bellevue House, with the Sons of Khepri's bloody heart superimposed on top. Social media exploded with questions about Bellevue House and speculation on who was behind the ads. Posts on both sides of the issue numbered in the thousands. Some praised the decision to raze the house, saying that to erase a history of genocide was no loss, and that it was necessary to healing. Others decried it as a political correctness run wild, another concession to the strident social justice mobs.

We were nowhere near ready to take the plan public; it went public anyway. For all the backroom secrecy, real or imagined, some leak or puncture in the seal had let the rumours out into the cyclonic churn of the media. The same night the posters appeared, the news was full of it: Bellevue House was to be demolished, the entire structure bulldozed and the site redeveloped into a new initiative, ostensibly to benefit the city.

Following the leak, the official statement from City Hall was as vague as we could get away with, which only fuelled speculation. I heard that Bellevue House had been purchased by a Chinese tech conglomerate for use as a digital innovation hub. I heard it would be turned into a Canadian flagship location for a Mexican-restaurant chain from the States. I heard it would be converted into a mosque, at the behest of a Saudi prince looking for reasons to invest in Canadian wind power. I heard Avril Lavigne had bought it as a retreat. The obvious and fair choice was to turn it into an Indigenous cultural centre. (Which is what some of us always had in mind, no matter what the papers say.)

There were inevitable questions about costs for the taxpayer, implications for cultural heritage, zoning laws, bird migration routes. But City Hall insisted that the matter was too important to delay — the house's time in history had passed, and both Parks Canada, who helped administer the site, and the City of Kingston agreed that a new narrative was needed to move forward in unity. It was necessary to acknowledge the hard facts: Sir John A. Macdonald had starved Indigenous people to herd them onto reserves, his residential school system leaving a legacy of broken families, languages lost, children beaten and abused. And never mind the lurid rumours going around about his firstborn son, the one who died at Bellevue House.

Opinions poured forth. Statements came from the university, the military college, Corrections workers, the coach of the Kingston Frontenacs junior hockey team. Newscasters rushed to get reactions from local businesses, academics, economists, activists, students on the street. Everyone had an opinion, though no one knew exactly what was happening.

It was around then that I saw the two women for the first time — the ones who'd later confirm my ugliest fears. They were both interviewed on the six o'clock news, given the same question: *What does Bellevue House mean to you?*

The first, wearing a grey parka and thick leather mitts, was identified onscreen as *Mary Tegan, Tyendinaga Mohawk.* "It's time to acknowledge Macdonald's true legacy and to stop celebrating him," she said. "For me, for my people, every time we walk by Bellevue House, it's a reminder of all the damage he did."

I didn't catch the second woman's name. She was hunched and hugging herself in the cold, wearing a yellow kerchief tied around her head. When the reporter asked her the question, she looked at the camera, and there was a drill boring into her eyes, some poison tip headed for her core that was too deep to be stopped.

"Bellevue House is a piece of our *history!*" she said, spitting out the words. "To rip it down is an outrage! A goddamn outrage!"

The problem was, I believed them both. I believed that Mary Tegan lived with wounds passed down directly from Macdonald's hand. As for the second woman, I'd seen people gnash over hundreds of different injuries. I'd seen sorrow and fear and suspicion that grows over months, like a strangling vine. But I'd never seen someone mad like this. It was unnatural. Inhuman, almost. She had the certainty of the possessed.

That's when I started to understand that the barriers were collapsing between us and something inconceivable. I hadn't named it yet. Had no idea what specific horror was to come. But I could feel time buckling, in the rhythm of a sickness throbbing just below the surface of the world.

5. A house is a house and a devil's a devil. Until it's not. The smell of the gun is so natural to me now, like a vapour I can wear as skin by oiling the muzzle with my bare hands, to shield myself from the pest. But it wasn't always like this. So much is fluid — permeable in ways we can't fathom — but in some things, before and after are irreconcilable states.

The bomb threat on City Hall came on a Monday morning in mid-December. I was at my desk, trying not to look out the window at the flags. The screech of the alarm was so abrupt and jarring that I jumped in my chair and spilled coffee all over my hands. The scalding heat felt angry, and I was angry, too, at yet another drill, another false emergency.

I knew it was real when there was a commotion in the hall, everyone heading for the exits, voices clipped and nervous. I shuffled out of my office and into the cold with the rest of them like a dazed cow, empty of will. I tried not to hear the whispers running through the crowd, the cursed sibilants, "terrorists" and "explosives" and "house." Somehow I knew that events would start moving much faster now.

That afternoon, police in riot gear cordoned off the blocks around City Hall and arrested a Syrian man who peddled trinkets from a rug in Market Square. I'd never spoken with him, but I was sorry to see him go: I knew he had nothing to do with the threat.

✕

You have to be careful with certain terms. Search "bomb" and "schematic" and "fertilizer" in succession and men in dark suits start taking note. CSIS, FBI, Interpol. You become a person of interest, a potential threat, and one day the black SUVs show up at your curb, carrying agents who want to know if you have a pressure cooker in your cupboard or a copy of the Qur'an on your bookshelf.

Likewise, some words can betray you. Words like *house* and *family*, *career* and *nation*. They aren't as stable as they seem; their structures can collapse, faster than you'd think. And you're never sure who owns them — these words and the lives they attach to. You never know who's found the controls to the system, and might decide on a whim to take the solid truths you know and rearrange the molecules. Who might use these words to systemize their own madness. To condemn people for generations. Seduce them into death. Destroy lasting love.

It only happened that once, with Sandra. I was sitting in the living room, watching the Sons of Khepri's TV spot air for the hundredth time. For weeks, I'd been distracted by a festering sound underneath everything, like the buzzing of a massive hive. I couldn't stop thinking about Macdonald's son — how he'd died, and why. What a mad variety of atrocities his father had engineered, and what others he might have been capable of. What cruelty is at the foundation of all we do, all we are.

Sandra came into the living room and kneeled in front of me, putting her hand on my knee.

"Tim," she said, looking at the screen. "You can't keep going like this. We can't."

Tim. Timothy Gant. Husband and father. City Councillor. So much erased in one moment of lost control. Base, animal instinct. Reptilian brain.

"Whatever it is you've done —"

I remember the tingle in my palm after it connected with her jaw. The moment I took to stare at my hand before reaching to help my wife up off the floor. How detached I felt from it, as though it was something I'd watched happen on TV.

Eleanor came to see what the noise was. The air in the room smelled of oil and furniture polish. We all looked at one another and pretended to be confused, jarred out of reality for a spell by some malicious invisible actor. But all of us knew what had happened, parents and child alike. We all knew, in that moment, that there are some truths you can't come back from.

6. The Sir John A. Macdonald memorial statue stands in the southeast corner of City Park, about two blocks from where I used to live. Cast in bronze and perched on a pedestal of pink marble, the man they called Old Tomorrow clutches a scroll in his right hand and stares dolefully out across King Street, in the direction of the Celtic cross that marks where Irish died by the hundreds in the fever sheds while he hid out at Bellevue House, conjuring abominations.

On the night I hit Sandra, I stood before the statue, waiting in vain for answers. Who were the Sons of Khepri, and what noxious force was backing their campaign to bury us? What strange ministry had emerged to defend Macdonald's legacy? What goal could possibly be served by preserving Bellevue House any longer? At the time, I still believed that, whatever the means, for some of us — for me — there was nobility in our intention to take it down and build something better. All the shady kickbacks and engineered outrage in the world couldn't change that.

There were no answers at home and no answers from statues. But there was one place I hadn't looked yet. From City Park I walked along Stuart Street, through the campus, past the hospital and up University Avenue to the Douglas Library. None of the official histories would have what I was looking for; no plaque or proclamation would speak of it. My hope lay in the university's Special Collections, housed on the second floor of Douglas, the old limestone giant.

Inside, I requested dozens of volumes, poring over arcane histories and yellowed pamphlets, searching for words that trilled with hidden menace. As I read, moving from book to book, page to page, I found only bits, tiny flecks of meaning that confirmed little. A death notice for Macdonald's infant son mentioned a closed-casket funeral. A blurry photograph showed Macdonald at City Hall, wearing a pin on his lapel that looked to be in the shape of a heart. There were stories of him disappearing for days at a time and returning to Parliament speaking gibberish, behaviour blamed on his legendary drinking. But nothing concrete, no revelation.

I was almost ready to admit defeat when I picked up a heavy leather-bound tome and found, underneath, the slim booklet that would chew me to pieces.

It was the colour of dried amber and no bigger than a postcard. The cover was plain, bearing only the title — *Hymns to the Roach of Khepri* — and an eerily familiar image of a bloody heart sprouting cilia-covered legs and two long, curled antennae. When I opened it, the text was incomprehensible, tiny runes that didn't seem organized according to any logical system or order. It wasn't until the words began to move that I understood.

All at once, as though triggered by an inaudible whistle, the bits of text began scrabbling like tiny beetles across the page. Their movements were a coordinated churn, a language that taught me to read it as I watched. I like to think it's because, by then, I was ready to see the repugnant truth. Moving through stories in a strange, whispering cadence, the insect text revealed the full extent of its sacrilege:

> The beast has gone by many names. Leech of the
> Eons. Heart of the Ages. Im-Dzha'ggon'. The Scarab of
> Malice. Scum Locust, Shadow Roach, Black Organ of
> the Old Ones: Nssu-Gh'ahnb — a creature out of time
> and space, so horrible that to gaze on it is to test the
> bounds of sanity. It has always been there, outside of
> time. Only with the right invitation, the proper ritual,
> is it able to cross the boundary into our world. Only

through the work of a dark priesthood willing to feed
its heinous appetite. Only by the sacrifices of its Sons.

As I sat, receiving the truth, the air around me turned thick and putrid. Fear writhed like a worm in my gut. I tried to move, to recoil from the cursed book that traced the path of the roach's malignant juice from the very origin of the country to the TV spots the Sons of Khepri were currently running twice every half hour. But my limbs were frozen, mired to immobility in the viscid atmosphere. My eyes bulged and my heart tripped as the bugs streamed off the pages and up my useless arms. I couldn't move, but I could feel, on my skin, the tickling of a million tiny legs, as they crawled up my neck and over my chin and into my nostrils and through my clenched lips, wriggling. They hit my eyes and I felt a gnawing pain, and then nothing at all.

When I came back to myself, I was somehow down by the water, behind the treatment plant on King Street, staring at a stripe of reflected moonray on the waves and the blinking red lights of the turbines across the river on Wolfe Island. When I turned around, the roiling sky and everything beneath it hit me like a bolt to the skull, an electrical shock. On the grass sloping up toward the road, on the street and sidewalk, hundreds of ghosts staggered in weightless despair, echoes of the people who had walked here and had their world taken away. I staggered and had to kneel. But the barrelling clouds called me forward. I got up and walked away from shore, navigating my way through the apparitions, up Centre Street, to the long green fence that marks the grounds of Bellevue House. I turned right, through the gate, past the Visitor Centre and through the trees. The house rose up before me, cast turquoise in the lunar light.

On the golden steps, at the top of the iron railing, he stood—Old Tomorrow himself. This time, it was no scroll he clutched, but a child wrapped in a woolen blanket, pinned with a brooch that I recognized too well: the heart of the Sons of Khepri. Macdonald's eyes blazed up at the white moon, and a dense clicking noise like the riffling of cards issued from his bulbous nose. A black shadow danced on his lips, and slowly there emerged from between them, black and glistening, the horned head of a giant cockroach. It loosed itself, skittered up his arm, and plunged its mandibles into the flesh of the child's bare neck, dribbling blood mixed with a black, oily secretion, a glyph of death daubed on its skin.

And that's where comfort ended, for me.

7.

Let's say Sir John A. Macdonald killed his firstborn son. Let's say he gave the child as a sacrifice to a god he couldn't articulate but which ruled him nonetheless—an ancient thing from beyond space and time, cultivating devotion in the powerful and merciless of the Earth. Let's say Macdonald raised up his child in the light of the larval moon and let the ravenous pest consume him.

Is that any worse than the truths we know?

It depends on which version of the story you believe.

×

It's around halfway through the movie when the script diverges so wildly from reality that it becomes a different story altogether.

We're back in the mayor's office with Staughton, Webb, and Gant. This time there's no whiskey. The mayor has no suit jacket on; Gant has his tie loosened and is sweating profusely. Only Tyson Webb keeps his DiCaprian cool, looking, the whole time, as though he's about to wink at the camera.

"Well, gentlemen," says the mayor. "Shall we commence the discussion about how utterly fucked we are? I told you, categorically, that if word of the plan got out, they'd *destroy* us. Now here we are: dog shit on the bottom of the public shoe. Webb, care to shimmy your frat-boy ass out of this one? It was you I recall saying, 'It's covered,' yes?"

Webb smiles but says nothing, and any lingering sympathy for pathetic little Tim Gant teeters into the void of Tyson Webb's silence.

"We have to renege," says Gant in a nasally voice, making his infamy complete. "We have to cancel the deal. We can't risk provoking these people—"

"What people? You know who's behind all this, do you?" yells the mayor. "You got something to tell us, Gant?"

"No! I mean, no. I don't know who they are. But they obviously have power. What if we can't beat them? We have to renege."

"So much for your stake in the public good, eh?" says the mayor. "And are you going to tell the CEO of Zocalar about a little twist in our plans? Eh? What makes you think he won't flay your nutsack faster than you can say *five for embezzlement?*"

"They'll turn the public against us!" says Gant. "This city isn't ready for so much change—"

"Fuck the city!" says the mayor. "I won't—"

There's the sound of a throat being emphatically cleared, and the camera pans to Tyson Webb. He appears calm and righteous, lit to shine.

"Boys," he says. "I suggest we stop the bickering and get down to business."

"The worthless taint speaks!" snaps the mayor. "What business? What other fucking business is there? Enlighten me, Webb. What could possibly require our attention beyond the entire fucking world collapsing on top of us?"

Webb smiles, slow and slick. "That depends who you mean by 'us,' Jim."

There's a terrible pause as the mayor's face goes red and his eyes balloon and his fists curl up into hard little walnuts of rage.

"You dickless weasel!" yells the mayor, jabbing his finger, getting right up into Webb's face. "What do you think about me checking your candy-ass into solitary at Collins Bay? I still have that authority, goddamn it!"

"I don't think so, Jim," says Webb, a smile sauntering across his face like a sly millipede. "I don't think you understand how little truth there is to that statement."

At this point, in the film, Webb snaps his fingers, and the big wooden doors to the office bust open to disgorge a swarm of federal officers in riot gear. They stamp in and surround Jim Staughton and Tim Gant, pistols drawn. Downey Jr. is the first to put up his hands—again, a subtle nod to his essential moral complexity, the trace of goodness in him that allows his redemption later in the story.

Tim Gant, not-Buscemi, just follows suit. Hapless, guilty, loathsome, weak.

The cops slap cuffs on both of them. The strings well up over triumphant timpani rolls as the camera pans to Tyson Webb, riot police spreading out like black wings around him. The music stops and we cut to a close-up of his blue-eyed celebrity face.

"Now," he says. "Here's how it's going to be."

×

Here's how it's going to be.

Those are Hollywood words. No one says them out loud, not in real life, not the way they do in the movies. Real life can get lost on the cutting room floor, though. It gets buried under myth. Warped and changed.

In real life, Tim Gant had a spine. He came to that second meeting shaken, filled with dread after his nightmare of a statesman gone mad. Filled with conviction, too, that Bellevue House *should* be knocked down. Determined to make the case for its demise, knowing what black dreams lived like fungus within its walls.

In real life, Tyson Webb showed up to City Hall that day wearing a pin in the shape of a heart, and I knew right away that I'd misread everything. That our paths had diverged, and that the road Webb was on led to a place he'd sold his soul to reach. In real life, there was no big public trial for corruption, with Robert De Niro as the crown attorney. In real life, I negotiated a plea deal that kept me out of prison, but killed my chances at holding public office, or maybe any job, ever again. In real life, I went back to my family with my head hung like a guilty, furious dog.

In the movie, I went down hard. In real life, things were much, much worse.

8. When the public announcement came out of City Hall, it was worded as a personal statement from the mayor: a confident, almost lusty reassertion that Bellevue House was to be demolished, its ghosts banished to the trash pile of history. A plaque would be erected on site to note that the house had been there, and had been significant. But plans would proceed as scheduled.

If the missive also hinted at some cowardice or weakness of heart on the part of the mayor's office — a grace note to set the scene for the performance to follow — I wouldn't know: I couldn't bring myself to read the full release.

I do, however, remember the following day, when the real Tyson Webb appeared on television for his first big press conference. Dressed in a shiny grey suit and a crisp blue tie pinned with a tiny golden scarab that most people probably didn't notice, Webb presided over a crowd gathered under the grand arches of Memorial Hall, fingers jutting with purpose, expressing with palpable scorn his absolute disgust at the corruption that had taken root in the office of the mayor. He explained how, working closely with local police and the OPP, he'd brokered his way into the mayor's inner circle to witness first-hand the disregard for the rule of law on wanton display in the crooked deal with the powerful Montreal development firm Zocalar. He listed our offences in clinical detail, decrying our cynicism and blatant disrespect for the genuine spirit of reconciliation that had been exploited to line the pockets of political elites. He made a point of implicitly laying the whole swindle on the back of one shameless councilman who had abused his privilege for personal gain. Finally, Webb vowed to fight back, demanding a formal inquiry and pledging to personally spearhead an initiative to clean up backroom dealings at City Hall.

As to the fate of Bellevue House, all plans would be put on hold until further notice, to ensure the process could proceed untainted by the toxins of greed and ambition.

Social media exploded again, and the papers published shocked headlines, and pundits across the country weighed in during the dinnertime news broadcasts. The names Jim Staughton and Timothy Gant were dragged through a mud so thick and black it could have swallowed up the sun. As the story progressed, attacks focused increasingly on the latter name—a young, privileged upstart with great potential, turned by his essential moral bankruptcy into a simpering twit, a devious rat, a man both wretched and despicable. His name became a shorthand for everything that was wrong with the system, every good intention made leprous with selfishness and hate.

Meanwhile, Tyson Webb emerged as a favoured candidate in the upcoming mayoral election, a political chrysalis heading for glorious rebirth.

✕

The last meal my family and I ever ate together was a roast I over-cooked until it was hard and shrivelled as a giant pill bug. It was February, the hard part of winter, when calls for me to resign were at fever pitch. We sat around the table in the dining room, smooth jazz playing in the background, as though everything was normal and fine. No one said much, until the ad for Bellevue House came on the radio.

"Crooked bureaucrats wanted to destroy it..."

Since Tyson Webb had worked his sorcery, preserving the house in the name of fairness and justice while forfeiting his soul to the vermin within, its fame had grown by bounds. People came by the hundreds to take selfies standing out front. At the Parks Canada Visitor Centre, they added a souvenir kiosk that sold postcards and tea towels and T-shirts with John A. Macdonald's face in iconic Canadian red, in both *PIONEER* and *MURDERER* versions. The city's culture office announced a summer concert series to be held on-site, which the radio had been advertising around the clock.

Still: I'd never considered that my own blood might get roped in.

Eleanor, pushing pellets of meat around her plate, cocked her head and angled her shoulder forward, like she always did when she wanted something.

"Dad," she said. "Do you think you could get tickets to that thing? Through your...connections?"

I tried to stay calm. At least, I want to think I did. Either way, I looked at my nine-year-old daughter too hard, my eyes already hexed with the knowledge that the roach was out there, listening.

"Let me be extremely clear," I said. "I don't want you anywhere *near* that place. Erase it from your mind. It's dangerous. Cursed, even. Don't speak of it again. Forget it exists. Understand?"

I noticed that I was pointing my fork at her. I expected her to be a bit shocked, maybe even a bit afraid—I wanted her to be afraid—but instead, she just frowned and gave a half shrug.

"Bobby said you probably wouldn't be able to," she almost sneered. "Since you got disgraced."

"Who the fuck is Bobby?"

"Tim!" said Sandra, in the middle of chewing a bite of roast like a plug of tobacco. Her hands were shaking, fork clinking against the side of her plate. My wife was a professor of economics, a hardened academic who'd paid her own way through school bartending at the city's worst clubs. I almost never saw her rattled.

Eleanor looked at her mother. "Mom, can I be done?"

Sandra nodded, still looking at me.

I pushed back my chair and followed Eleanor to the living room, wary of the threat I exuded but too agitated by her mention of Bellevue House to care. She sat and faced the TV. I grabbed her chin and turned her face toward mine so I could look into her eyes. I needed to see: Did Hell have her, too?

"Look," I said. "I don't give a shit what Bobby says, whoever he is. He's right. I lost my job. I paid the price. But that's beside the point. Do not go near that house. Do you understand? DO NOT GO FUCKING NEAR IT."

"Dad," she said, her voice meek again. "You're squeezing too hard."

I let her go. She gave me a confused look, then shifted her gaze behind my shoulder, to where her mother stood, watching.

×

The thing is, you never stop loving them. No matter how far gone you get—how deep into the bog of fear and dread that separates our world from the ones beyond, how crushed by the pressure of your own obsessions—there's always a place in which you are only ever loving them. You love them for what they are and what they're not. You love them even if they betray you. You'd kill anyone who was trying to harm them, even if it only meant they'd live on to hurt you more, in the end. That's just the way it is.

You never stop loving them. Even after they leave.

9. I eat boxed meals now. Kraft Dinner. Takeout pizza. Sticky orange chicken from the Chinese place down the street. I polish the gun, count the rounds. Look every so often at the contraption in the corner. Wires and timers. Fuses and dials. Gelatin and putty. Borax and bleach. It will take a lot of explosives to destroy the roach. If it's even possible. It's huge now, tumescent, its strength built up over months of feasting on fresh blood.

Because that's the thing about growing a monster.

You have to feed it.

✕

It was about a week after I finally resigned—the same week Sandra took Eleanor to her mother's house in Gananoque—that the new campaign started.

At first, it was just a few ads in the *Whig-Standard*, solid black rectangles with nothing inside but the words *INVESTING IN OUR HERITAGE*, above the tiny icon that had shifted ever so slightly from a broadly cardiac shape to something more arthropod in nature. These drew little attention.

Much more controversial were the billboards that went up along Princess Street, showing Bellevue House wreathed in a halo of yellow light, with the same insectoid graphic superimposed on top and large, ecstatic lettering beneath proclaiming, *BELLEVUE HOUSE: A NEW FRONTIER*.

The CBC aired its first news story in March, a mini-documentary about a new virtual reality project on the house and its history. By then, social media was lit up, chewing the cud of the house's journey from cruelty to redemption with a thousand hot takes and retweets.

The big TV spot started airing around Easter. It had been crafted to appear random—the work of some overpriced agency full of marketing gnats, no doubt—but the tells were there, if you knew where to look.

The ad began with a close-up of candles being lit, the lilting murmurs of a choir. This sound built gradually, in layers, one voice piling on top of another until the vocal melody kicked in and became identifiable as a full-blown choral version of the Tragically Hip's "Ahead by a Century." The camera pulled back to reveal the singers, four rows of angelic young men and women in white robes, each holding a lit candle bearing a tiny version of the icon of the heart of plague. The kicker, of course, was that they weren't performing in the apse of St. Mary's Cathedral, or on the stage of the Grand Theatre—but on the green, L-shaped portico and golden front steps of Bellevue House.

As the choir reached its crescendo, text appeared on screen, aligned to cut straight across the robes of the singers in the bottom row. *THE NEW BELLEVUE HOUSE*, it said. *TRANSCEND*. It was all too easy to miss the fine print at the bottom, stating that the ads had been paid for by the Sons of Khepri.

The spot created a frenzy in the media. A few reporters who still had their integrity looked askance at Tyson Webb, who had, after all, come to fame as the house's champion. But that story already had its villain. And besides, by then, it was hard to say how much control we all had left. The roach feeds off outrage and zeal in equal measure, and if it all seemed to ramp up too fast, with too much urgency—well, that was a tell, too.

×

In its notoriety, Bellevue House became more and more of a symbol—of new beginnings, stories seen through changed eyes. Its Facebook page gained thousands of followers. The CBC produced a podcast about it. A local rock band mentioned it in a hit song. It spawned a series of trading cards, a coffee table book, a flurry of apps.

There was one further protest—organic, as far as I knew, or impossible to tell otherwise. A group of Indigenous activists gathered outside the gates on Centre Street, holding placards that reminded people what had started this whole thing in the first place: the murderous policies that Sir John A. Macdonald had crafted and enforced, the continued veneration of him a painful reminder of how little Canada understood of the pain that Indigenous people had suffered. The unspoken fact of his alleged infanticide. They wanted Bellevue House demolished, according to the original plan. Within a few hours, police had shown up to escort them into white vans, to shuttle them to an undisclosed location set aside specifically for public protest by Indigenous people. Online uproar was confined to a few radical corners of Twitter.

The wave of love and fascination with the house continued. Articles followed videos followed poems. Before long, the legend of Bellevue House had inspired so many opinions, ideas, and pledges of devotion or disdain that the physical fact of it became of less and less concern.

So it was almost anticlimactic when, three months after the election that had brought Tyson Webb to power in a landslide victory over the incumbent Jim Staughton, a wrecking ball took the first chunk out of the eastern wing. Within three days, a pack of bulldozers had destroyed Bellevue House, leaving only a deep hole in the earth and a fug of carbon and sulphur hovering above it like a shit-specked poison mushroom cap.

Bellevue House — the first one — was gone.

A week later, construction began.

10. Yesterday, I stepped on a mouse chewing on a pizza box in the corner, ground it into a slurry of bone and pink guts, an ambiguous blotch with few hints of the animal's natural shape. Mice, when you crush them, die.

With roaches, you can't always be sure.

It's hard to be sure of anything, these days, unless you have the courage of faith. I've come to see this apartment, shithole that it is, as a hall of government of a different kind. I am its lone councillor, its arbiter and whip. I drink cold vodka and listen for the heartbeat in my chest. I wonder how deep into me the roach has already burrowed.

If life can be transformed so utterly, without one's control, is it not inevitable that a new idea of the world will follow?

×

When the Bellevue House Cultural Learning Pavilion opened that spring, crowds came out in record numbers.

In every superficial detail, the Pavilion was identical to its predecessor. It had the same L-shaped floor plan, same white stucco walls and terracotta roofs, same pillars and shutters painted dark hunter green, same sunburst of colour on the golden front steps. But now, where the Visitor Centre had been, there was a bulletproof ticket kiosk, manned by a clerk dressed in black fatigues, a heart-of-plague badge on his shoulder, collecting the entry fee of $39.95. This admission entitled you to walk through the fabled gates and through the woods, to emerge in view of the new, historic replica complex erected in the exact spot on which Bellevue House — the first one — had stood. Outside the front doors, a plaque explained the significance of the site. How the original had been built in 1840, by a merchant named Charles Hales. How it was one of the first examples of the Italian Villa style in Canada. How it had briefly housed the first prime minister of Canada. And how, now, thanks to Mayor Tyson Webb's Heritage Revitalization Committee, and in partnership with Utheca, a development firm from Calgary, the site had undergone a complete and total restoration program, which, at minimal expense and maximum benefit to the taxpayer, would allow for the next chapter of its history to unfold, as a lynchpin of waterfront beautification, a centre for the university's New Lenses research program, and an educational museum and theme park for public enjoyment and civic pride.

On opening day, the crowd was thick, agitated, and damp. It

was near the back of the line that I saw the two women again, the ones who'd answered the question: *What does Bellevue House mean to you?* This time, they both had on matching yellow kerchiefs, to go with the twinned looks of rapture on their faces. There was a strange energy in their posture, as though they'd been filled with some volatile fuel. Both of them were craning their necks and almost twitching, eyes beaming wide and fevered toward the ticket kiosk up ahead.

Seeing them made my blood pound in my temples. I had an irresistible urge to talk to these women, to ask them why they were here, what they hoped to attain. To warn them. Elbowing through the crowd, I made my way over to them.

"Hey," I said. "You two."

They turned to me with looks of bliss on their faces, foreheads beaded with sweat.

"I saw you on TV one night," I said. "When this all started."

"Isn't it beautiful?" the white woman said, her eyes focused on something far away. "I'm so happy. So happy for this house." All of her rage had evaporated into stunned bliss.

"What happened?" I said to the other woman, the one named Mary. "Before, you hated this place." I knew; she knew. The question was futile, already answered. She smiled at me, wide and full of joy.

"We're all its children now," she said. "Aren't we?"

I wanted to argue with her, to slap her awake; but the crowd had taken on its own life, everyone pushed in directions we couldn't control, and the two women drifted away from me, eyes fixed once again on the barbed spire of the Pavilion.

That was enough to convince me for good. I clenched my jaw and dug my nails into my palms and walked away from Bellevue House as fast as I could, pushing through the crowds that were advancing on the gates, thinking through how every good thing in my life had been twisted away from me like limbs wrenched from a butchered carcass. The public abandoning me, then the people I loved. Tyson Webb reared up in my brain, and I saw a cold black mandible jammed into his spine, making him into a puppet of an insectoid hunger too loathsome to comprehend.

I got away, but my escape from the Pavilion was bittersweet. In that moment, I realized that to halt the infection — to stop the creature for good — I'd have to walk into its mouth.

11. Everyone knows the rest. Tyson Webb's memoir has sold close to a million copies worldwide, the public swallowing every lie like a handful of butter-slicked popcorn. The seven-figure movie deal was inevitable, with Webb on board as an executive producer, bringing financing from the CBC, the City of Kingston, the Province of Alberta, and Sons of Khepri, Inc. The film premiered at Cannes, to much critical acclaim. By last month, when the Academy Awards were telecast, the fictional Tyson Webb, as played by Leo DiCaprio, was already more recognizable than the real man.

When Webb went up to accept his Best Picture statue, he gave a long and impassioned speech about the need to embrace change and new ways of thinking, and flashed a Canadian flag, which drew cheers and applause. A few fashion columnists remarked on his unusual brooch, a vaguely arthropod symbol one might mistake for a heart. But Hollywood expects flamboyance. In the end, the film took eleven statues and claimed its place in the canon of great political dramas.

×

I keep very little now. The couch where I sleep. A small table for my laptop. The rifle and rounds. The vest and its payload. I watch the movie again and again and again, and brood on the rhythm in my chest. I curse and condemn the ancient foulness that gestates beneath the pavilion, waiting for its Sons to summon it fully across the dimensional veil, and commit myself to Nssu-Gh'ahnb's extermination.

It's time for my version of the story. I understand that it's impossible to exhume one definitive truth from the tangle of shadows. In speaking out, I'd be called insane. But I've felt the roach's karma, its oily cilia brushing the back of my neck. The dirt stench of its insect's blood. Its fetid heartbeat taking over my own. I've known and shared secrets with the vile disciples who feed it with the bodies and souls of those living under their dark dominion. We are all its children now. So where does paranoia end and the Pavilion begin? How deep are the cracks in the surfaces we think are solid? Sometimes even I have trouble separating the truth from what happened in the movie.

I imagine a news anchor throwing to a clip from the film — Tim Gant, the pathetic character with the greasy hair and the mewling voice. I imagine footage of charred wood and contorted metal and brick turned to dust, a black mist dissipating over the rubble. I try to imagine my face hovering like a moon above the chaos. But I see only his face — the man from the screen, the man who was never me, until he was.

The creature might not let me get through the doors. It might smell the cleansing whisper of explosives, the sour milk stench of my fear. Even if I do get inside, hidden in the crowd, the pest will still be invisible. Still *behind*. I won't be able to see it, to know where to point my gun, or where to stand when I push the button.

But I will feel the plague-heart's pulse. I will know the roach is there. And I will get as close as I can. As close as I can.

Inquisition (Extended Mix)

From the opening notes, he recognizes the tune.

It takes a few seconds to build. Low, droning synth, like a muezzin murmuring prayer. A percussive, bullet-spray rasp. Growling guitar, the grinding of tanks on bones.

At about thirty seconds, the beat kicks in.

The door creaks open. He hears bootsteps through the burlap. The hood is ripped off and he is slapped across the face, a dark sting, a ringing light. Curses barked into his ear. He is the worst of insects. *Fucking dirty traitor.* Slapped again. Slapped again.

The world spins. The guard, task accomplished but never complete, tugs the hood down over his face, the rough material scraping his skin, ripping hairs from his matted beard. Again he is shrouded, suspended in brown blindness. He hears bootsteps leaving. The door slams closed.

This is routine.

He sags, trying to go to the silent place. Pinpricks sizzle on his eyelids, a frenzied mosh. His weight tugs against the ropes chafing his wrists. He tastes blood in his mouth, wiggles a loose molar with his tongue. He's given them no names, condemned no brother—not out of any loyalty so much as a final desire to tie off the violence at himself. Absorb all of the punishment that his bones and muscle can bear.

In assent with his wish, they turn up the volume.

The song is Skinny Puppy, "Inquisition." Off the *Last Rights* album. But not, exactly. An extended mix, from a bonus seven-inch single. It differs considerably from the original: the intro is drawn out, there's more space between the beats. A long break in the middle where the words give way to synth babble, minimalist claustrophobia — the music left hanging, flailing in the void, no structure to anchor its relentless rhythms.

The album version is more concise. More staccato. In truth, he thinks, it would make better torture music.

He braces for the vocal. Ogre, groaning:

"Bla-tant-ant-ant...Man-ner-er-er..."

Things could have been different, if only he'd hidden the records better.

✕

He remembers buying the first one.

Back then he was just Amir. He'd gone to Marché du Disque on Mont-Royal in search of Nirvana albums. He was combing the racks, cautiously fingering a Ministry CD, when the clerk, a scrawny white guy with thick-rimmed glasses, came over and gave him a look: *I see potential here.*

"Try this," he said, handing over the plastic jewel case locked in an anti-theft sleeve, a nightmare wrapped in cellophane and stickered at $15.99. The effect was instant: that terrifying circus on the cover, temples and mausoleums, death's heads and gargoyles, toxic yellow mountains in the background, the whole mad landscape overlaid with unhinged spider script — *SkiNNy PUppy*. Everything about it designed to make you squirm.

He thought back to the day at school the week before. He'd been walking down the hall of Académie de Roberval, thinking about the Habs game that night. Unprepared to see the word gouged into his locker with a pen knife — *RAGhead*. He felt it like a gut-punch. When he turned around, the kids were standing there. Older by a year. Arms crossed, leaning against the wall, glowering.

"Better watch out," said one with a squared-off bowl cut. "Open season on camel jockeys." He tossed a scrap of yellow ribbon that flitted down to rest at Amir's feet.

He'd wanted, so badly, to rage back. Ram his fist into the metal of his locker until it buckled and the slur on it became unreadable. Ram his fist into bowl cut's jaw until his teeth shattered. Instead, he went outside, shivering in the autumn cold. Saw the mouse dart out from a hole behind the door, scurry out into the light and freeze, its tiny nose twitching like a nubbin of black rice. It was a reflex more than anything—a place to throw his force, the heaving in him. He reached out and brought down his big black boot, grinding with a twist, feeling the mouse's bone structure collapse.

Later, cleaning the fur and blood off his sole, he'd felt sick to his stomach about it all. How much it mattered. How little.

How common it was, to kill something.

"You're gonna love it," the clerk said, grinning down at Amir as he gaped at the Skinny Puppy CD. "Trust me."

He knew, as he bought the record, what his father would think. *Trash. Western garbage.* Relished the blasphemy. Walked out feeling righteous and brave, in possession of a new stake in himself. On his way out the door, he spied the poster tacked to a corkboard by the exit: *SKINNY PUPPY.* Live at Le Spectrum, in just over a month's time. Laughed to himself. Who would he go with? His elation wavered and he breathed in to try and hang on to it.

Before going home, he wrapped the disc in his sweatshirt and stuffed it into the back pocket of his knapsack. He knew he'd need a good hiding place. If he hid it outside—in a bag under the steps in the apartment courtyard, say—he could pick it up on his way to school, listen to it on his scuffed Discman. But what if someone found it? What if it froze, got brittle, cracked? Besides, he wanted it within reach. To be able to take it out at night, plug in his headphones when he was supposed to be asleep, internalizing the music's fractured cadences.

In the end, he stuffed it in the back of his desk drawer under a sheaf of blank paper. Why would his father look there? He, who rarely looked at Amir at all these days except to scowl?

That night, after dinner, Amir sat at his desk, staring through his homework, feeling the energy of the record pulse up through the wood, the weird gravitational pull of its abominations. Knowing the music would always be part of him, now.

×

The floor shakes. Bass hammers his chest, buzzes in his cracked molars. He tries to spit, finds his mouth sawdust-dry.

They hit the strobe.

Light jitters through the burlap, pinging his retinas. It takes a huge effort to squeeze his eyes shut. A hot stink wheezes up from his mouth, sulphur and charred meat. He feels a familiar liquefying in the stomach.

Raking his ears, Ogre's dirty pig-sex growl: *"Bonding ce-ment no long-er holds-olds-olds . . ."*

Acid heat runs down his leg like a thin snake. He inhales the sickly-sweet smell of his own waste. Feels a rattling in his cheek-bones — something shattered. Retches. Twitches. Hang, hang; his eyes droop. Synths echo with the blood bubbling in his nose. The drums kick in again, the snare smacking wetly into his gut like a giant tongue.

The extended mix is track two on the *Inquisition* EP. Preceded by the radio edit and followed by "Lahuman8" and "Mirror Saw (Dub Mix)". The *Last Rights*–era material cemented Skinny Puppy's reputation as an uncompromising force for sonic brutality, while putting a new spin on its sound. The album even had a ballad, "Killing Game."

The information floats up from a dark place inside him, dislodged from forgotten fissures in his muscle, the cobwebbed cleft of his brain where all the minutiae of his old life still moulders, despite efforts at cleansing. Some things you cannot leave behind.

Here, in this place, everything about his background makes it worse for him. Mother of Chechen descent, raised in a Paris *banlieue*.

Father an Algiers man named Muhammed. And him? That's the greatest joke of all: in here, the nationality that would usually save him—his Canadian passport, blood of the West, his home and native land—is the wellspring of his deepest curse. Turncoat. Betrayer. Defecator on flags. Enemy Combatant.

Ogre.

"... wicked resenting never faces itself..."

He feels an urge prodding his chest like an anxious worm. Quells it with a swallow of dust. The music warps, begins to lose shape, liquefying everything, crawling between his different selves like veins of living dirt.

They turn up the volume.

✗

He became a collector.

It was true: the records were dark things. Drug addiction. Murder. Chemical warfare. Environmental ruin. Titles weird and askew, daring you to react: *Too Dark Park. VIVIsectVI. Cleanse Fold and Manipulate. Rabies. Bites. Last Rights.*

Over a month, he bought them all, moving on to EPs and singles once he'd exhausted the full-lengths, filling his desk drawer with a sizable chunk of the Skinny Puppy catalogue. By the time he got the *Inquisition* EP, the clerk at Marché du Disque knew him by name and they were sharing brief chats about best albums, favourite cuts. It was a dream for Amir—real talk. There was no one at school like this.

He knew he had to find a way to go the concert. Felt the pull of obsession, the desperate urge to dissolve into a crowd of people who wouldn't look at him and instantly see some video game Arab brandishing an AK. To be among others who'd had their lockers defaced. To see Ogre up close, wallow in the scouring force of his guttural rage.

He concocted a plan. He told his mother he wanted to go to a friend's house. For once, it was lucky she knew so little of his life. It didn't occur to her to ask, *What friend?* He knew she'd take the request to his father, begging the way she sometimes did—pleading, *Give him a chance.* He trusted she could convince his father, find a crack in his carbide shell, touch some hidden soft place in a soul that couldn't conceive of love in a city that was no home but was simply the least dangerous, the least cruel of all the places he'd landed. His father—not hardline in any particular way. Not especially religious. Just restless. Displaced. Angry.

It took two weeks of closed-door discussions. Amir listened from his own bedroom, one headphone on, pumping tinny beats into his ear to dull the sound of his father's yelling, the other ear free to hear well in advance if they were coming to his room, so he could quickly shove the Discman back into his crowded drawer. The CDs took up most of the space now. He'd need a new hiding place soon. But he kept putting it off, telling himself there was nothing to worry about. Secretly relishing his guilt. Edgy, anxious, he waited for his mother to come with the verdict.

Three days before the show, she put his steaming breakfast oatmeal down in front of him and said, "You can go."

She wanted a name, a phone number. He conjured one up from his delirium, foreign enough to be acceptable: *Nivek.* Said he didn't know the number. Said there was nothing to worry about. Nodded through her clipped questions, every pore leaching tiny beads of sweat, feeling his father's silence infuse the walls of the house from where he sat in the living room, staring down the day's *La Presse.*

It was the last time Amir ever hugged his mother.

✕

At times, he can hear music from other cells thumping through the walls. Weak stuff—Queen. Metallica. Even his brothers would know that for the sap it was.

None of them would know Skinny Puppy, though. As far as he knew, no other inmates here had his intimacy with the West, its enduring stain. With training, with prayer, he had tried to erase it from his soul—cleanse it with the balm of righteousness. Choked the voice of his past's questioning. Retained only the will, the gargoyle screams of his haunted youth.

He hears the crack of gunshots somewhere outside. Pictures a firing squad: ten white, camouflage-clad soldiers lined up, guns wedged against shoulders, barrels trained on a lone Arab muttering *Allāhu akbar*s into the eddying dust to honour the luck of his martyrdom and quell the fear he's not supposed to feel. Knows the so-called good guys aren't supposed to do such things—executions, et cetera—but feels the truth of the image anyway, the force of its judgment. They have their own righteousness, these infidels; sing their own hymns to death.

The prodding comes again, lumping up past his heart.

Wicked, wicked. Find an anchor in the darkness, Amir, or drown.

×

When he walked out the door, shoulder slung with a black canvas knapsack filled with spare clothes to keep up the sleepover ruse, the cold air on his face was like a baptism. The night sky was clear and starry, and he even felt a twinge of sentiment for the great white cross glowing atop the humped silhouette of Mount Royal.

The Metro ride, Parc to Place-des-Arts, took less than fifteen minutes. He walked up to Le Spectrum, praying the show wasn't sold out. The kiosk glowed like a squared moon in the winter dark. There wasn't even a line.

"One," he said. "Please." Slid his twenty-dollar bill through the circular opening in the glass like an offering. Then the ticket was in his hand, crisp and still warm from the printer. He was patted down by a monstrous security guard. When he strode into the main hall, the domed, purple-lit ceiling radiated toward him with the energy of a huge cosmic eye, the bass rumbling intestinally through the chasm of the room below.

The next two hours were a torture of anticipation while he waited for the band. A blur of fear and thrill and boredom, watching the roped-off nineteen-plus area, skulking in the shadow corners while the venue filled up with an army of black-clad ghosts with sparking, kohl-rimmed eyes.

When the lights fell and the room-shaking intro roared out of the sound system, it was like a bomb detonating in his chest. He clenched his hands, curled and uncurled his fingers. Tensed for an explosion of light.

When it hit, strafing the venue with a nuclear white pulse, he was there, on the stage—Ogre, in the flesh. Demon frontman in full froth, drizzled in grime and throwing cyborg dreadlocks around like tentacles of iron chain. Gnawing the poisoned meat of society, chewing all the anger and indignation into a mince, swallowing it while it choked him. Looking, to Amir, so much like a fallen god, ecstatic in his darkness, using it to be free.

He felt the push before he knew what was happening. The crowd like a knot of electrified muscle, peristaltic. In the space of three seconds he was hemmed in, tangled up in a snarl of young white boys in torn blacks, their lean, sweaty biceps jamming up against his own arms, slippery as raw chicken. Felt vertigo of his sneakers leaving the ground as the crowd surged forward, his body beginning to move without his say. His heart ratcheted up, his ears singing with a high fevered peal as he shut his eyes to shield them from the dollops of fake waste spraying out from the clanking stage. Before he could regain his balance, he was shoved face-first into the damp back of the skinhead beast in front of him. He breathed leather, saliva smearing his face. Nose crushed, mouth pressed, gasping. Smothered, suffocating. Flailing, praying: *savemesaveme*—

Just as he thought he'd black out, a little hand wedged between him and the choking leather to pry his chest free. The arm wrapped around his shoulders like a living cloud, warm, enveloping.

The memory so vivid.

The girl turns her face to his and smiles, supportive, sympathetic. A little embarrassed. Girds her hand against the leather wall that almost asphyxiated him and pries it forward, creating a pocket of safe space against the crowd's feral energy. He holds on to her, clasping the smooth, sweaty skin of her bare wrist, making a structure, a joint strength to withstand the surging. The air shakes with bass, smells of damp bodies and beer skunk and her clove-scented perfume.

"You okay?" she says, yelling over the music. He nods. Her skin has a dark cast to it, uncertain mocha. Hair like waves of black sand. The band ratchets up. The song: "Inquisition."

They stand, a scaffold of two sharing something soft and humane plucked from the bone-crunching noise. Watching silently as the band pummels through its set — vivisections, chemical warfare, drug addiction — holding hands until the concert ends and the last note drones out through Le Spectrum like the voice of a speared whale.

He turns to speak to her — say *thank you*, say *what's your name* — but before he can manage to, the girl squeezes his fingers and lets go and disappears into the stream of people slithering out the door.

By the time the lights come on, he's alone.

×

Alone, still. With Ogre. Hanging.

After his daily lullaby, they'll take him back to the cage. No praying. No talking to the brothers in other cages, lined up along the concrete like penned dogs, each waiting their turn. Tomorrow there might be questions. The day after, the same questions. The cruelties are getting more varied, ingenious. The only constants are boredom and, for some weeks now, the music.

Something stabs his kidneys, a spike of pain up his left side. They turn up the volume.

At times, he tries to remember the faces of the men he's hurt. Searches, grasping, for self-revelation, some holy light or shimmer of irrefutable truth in their dying eyes. Finds none. Only blood gush, entrails unspooling, desert blur, mealy brown darkness, handfuls of dry porridge crawling with ants shoved into his ragged mouth, the stench of his own waste—and now this dancefloor track from '92, slamming into his temples, keeping him awake forever. Loosening something inside.

×

It played out as an inevitability, as certain as a pledge of devotion.

He opened the front door with the ringing still in his ears, moved slow and quiet even though he could see the light on in the kitchen. When he turned into the doorway, his father was standing by the table, face flat and hard as a blade. The CDs were piled up in a metal bucket beside him. His mother stood behind, quiet, face buried in her scarf.

Amir stood, awaiting judgment. Accepted his martyrdom.

It was bad enough, his father said, that their son was turning into a do-nothing, a drug addict, wearing all black and moping all the time. Now he was listening to this toxic stuff? *Trash. Western garbage.*

His father grabbed him hard by the wrist and hauled him outside into the parking lot behind the building, lugging the garbage can in his other hand. Amir remembers the smell of lighter fluid, the bonechill of a Montreal sky gone black. Clothes still damp and sweaty from the show, frozen stiff. Skin slick, still tingling where the nameless girl had touched him.

He was made to pour the fluid on the CD cases, to empty the

whole bottle over the pyramid of cracked plastic, throw in the match and sit and watch the flames erupt and the oily fumes coil up into the air, wraithlike. Every record, single, EP — his whole collection. All the bleak, cleansing sounds he'd found solace in. Burning.

That night, lying in bed, nauseous from the stink, nursing a sharp headache, he had already started considering it. The possibility of a different way. Why just the old book and prayer and hypocrisy? If he was bound to rules, to past — denied love, whether from the strange girl who offered mercy or the father who couldn't — if he was *RAGhead*, irreparably, why not make a full commitment? There was war, anyway. There was always war. Kuwait, Algeria, Afghanistan. His father would encourage it. More study, more prayer. Had already said that religion might be the thing to *calm Amir down*.

If he couldn't have music, what might guide him instead?

×

Here is truth: there is nothing to confess that they don't already know. They saw him kill. Hero-slayer. Traitor. Now he hangs, baffled, lacerated, the rhythm kicking up into his chest, ribbitting at his throat, *wickedforcefedtorment*, bringing it all home.

The first man he tortured was Afghani, a shepherd. Accused of giving information to Canadian soldiers in Kandahar. He'd wanted to hide his face, but the brothers had made him show it, so the traitor would see exactly who'd come to dismantle him. "كندية," they said. *Canadian*. Cattle prods jammed into armpits, cigarettes sizzling flesh, a smell like cooked mutton, musky and sweet.

For a while, in captivity, he'd hung on. Retained the certainty of his faith. Clenched righteousness between his teeth like a metal plate, refusing to cede his grip even when they tugged at it. Days passed. Weeks. Months. Years? Time bled. Him beaten, near-drowned, threatened with dogs, hosed down cold and naked on the tile. *Allāhu akbar, Allāhu akbar.* Screaming at night, punches in the face, kicks in the shins. Cocks in his face, guns at his temple. Hot irons on his skin. Lights blazing and wrathful like cruel angels. Endless, deafening music.

The song approaches its clattering finale. He coughs, feels a surge, an eruption welling deep in his gorge, a molten ball of energy and plea. This one, he knows he can't neutralize. Somehow, now, he is Amir on both ends, infidel and martyr—but in the middle there is a different beast, a dumb, screaming soul that he cannot understand, cannot grasp, erase, or control, even though it's the thing in which all of his anger, pride, shame, confusion, and desire are born. The beast that sings. The blind one that likes music. Amir loves this music, this terrifying music at the irreconcilable core of him.

The worm in his chest swells and spasms up into his throat, splits him open, so when he finally breaks, it's not a river of cursed names leading to an ocean of blood, no renouncement of any creed, not with pathetic thrashing of limbs emaciated to bird weight—just the last tiny bit of himself left to give before he falls into the place where there are no pasts and he becomes the next version, gone mute in darkness. He sings, sings the last words in shredding ogre scream:

▓▓

Bootsteps through the burlap. The hood ripped off. Slapped again. Slapped again.

It was his favourite song, once.

Between the Pickles

i. You're just the Wrapper, Rosa. Just the Wrapper. That's what they told you. Your one job, your only job, is to wrap the sandwiches in waxed paper and slide them down the metal chute and that's it. Any problems and you're gone.

The thing stares out at her from between the two flaccid pickles like a hairless mouse. She caught it just as she was folding the first logoed flap over the spongy white bun, stopped short and gasped and summoned every bit of strength she had to stifle a shriek. Now she's just standing there, sweat soaking the back of her polyester uniform, every second that ticks by bringing her closer to the questions from her manager that she can't afford to answer. *What the hell is that? How did it get there?*

She wants, as bad as anything she's ever wanted, for the thing to be innocent, a rotten carrot or a stray piece of cattle bone that got missed in the grinding. But there's no mistaking it: the nail, the knuckle, the wavy lines of fingerprint, swollen and grey but still readable as the map of an individual body, maybe dead but maybe alive somewhere and wondering what became of its missing digit. Never dreaming that it would end up here, at Pancho's Escondido, nestled into the middle of an Azteca Burger with cheese, threatening to fuck up everything Rosa García has been working for over the past nine months.

Dios mío. Rosa feels hot acid rising up her gorge. She clenches her fists, presses fingernails into palms. Repeats the refrain in her head—the one they gave her, but also the longer one, the one she's made for herself, which she recites to keep her going whenever things look like they might start turning to shit again.

You're just the Wrapper. You're just the Wrapper, this is your only job. Focus on the paycheque, Rosa, hold it in your mind like the face of Jesus Christ, because it's the thing that's saving you. It's what's between you and *La Migra's* guns, searchlights whiter and hotter than the Chihuahuan noon, fear in your stomach like a heavy chain while you try not to breathe, try to stop existing for as long as it takes for them to move on to the scent of some other poor bastard cowering out there in the desert, half-dead from terror and thirst. It's the wall between you and the house back in Jalapa, Mama's bloody coughs rattling like wet bones in the kitchen, the smells of fever and rot and dust coming off her skin. It's protection from the sting of Angel's hand on your cheek when you cried for your dying mother.

Rosa thinks about Diego, back at the apartment, sleeping in his crib while Valentina watches the evening news beside him, as blissful and radiant a heaven as any holy book could promise.

The finger points at her, demanding a response. Even if it has nothing to do with her, even if it's just bad luck, it doesn't matter. *Illegal equals expendable.* Her manager's exact words. She'd had to look up *expendable*.

They'd have her on a southbound truck within an hour.

The hiss of a frozen patty hitting the griddle brings her back to present time. Like that, she decides. Don't move, don't breathe. Head down. Just like in the desert, let it pass you by.

Rosa swallows hard to settle her gorge and puts on her best company face — no problems here, *señor* — lifts the waxed paper over the nightmare to cover its horror with the friendly cow face of the Pancho's mascot, Vaca Loca, folds the greasy flaps under to seal the deal, and slides the sandwich down the metal chute and, she hopes, out of her life forever. She dings the bell, *order ready!*, and tries to fade back into the haze of frying oil and grill smoke filling the kitchen like a tropical mist.

Remember, Rosa. You're just the Wrapper.

2.

He's weighing how far to go.

It took considerable effort to suppress the initial gag reflex when he bit into it and felt the bone. To not panic once he drew it back and saw the thing buried in there, poking out just enough that it looked for all the world like his Azteca Burger was sticking out its tongue at him. To lift off the top bun and peel up the sour greyish flap that passed for a pickle and confirm what his incisors already knew: that there was a *human finger* in his lunch food, slathered in ketchup and Sombrero Sauce and a smattering of diced onions.

But what was absolutely heroic, absolutely fucking Herculean, was that Mike Stevens was *still* just sitting there looking at it, trying to decide on the best way forward. That he had the wherewithal to fight back disgust and take a rational look at the situation. To take a deep breath and imagine the kind of shit-show that would erupt, the kind of irreparable damage that would occur, if he were to stand up in the middle of the restaurant and scream like a baby and have to explain, first to the TV cameras and then to Head Office, that the beloved Pancho's chain was so lax in its food-handling practices that this grotesque tidbit had managed to travel from whatever cursed slaughterhouse it had come from, all the way down the delivery chain, to end up on his tray, in his burger, in his mouth.

Mike closes his eyes for a minute, running his fingers down the length of his tie, trailing grease. Everyone knows fourth-quarter revenues are dragging the bottom. Everyone's heard about what happened over at KBC-Flaxos after JerryBurger went tits up. If the axe falls at SitcoBVM, junior execs will be the first on the chopping block.

All that work, all that eating shit, all that proverbial licking of Carl Drais's ballsack, for nothing. The resort vacation over Christmas? Forget it. Never mind the family he and Kara have been talking about having, maybe a year down the road. All of a sudden he's *not father material*, just another dud in a bargain suit pleading his way through dozens of job interviews and eating Ritz Crackers and spreadable cheese for lunch.

Forget it. That's the thing to do. Forget it. Stand up, walk over to the trash, and dump the thing into the bin, erase it from memory. Take one for the team.

He opens his eyes and looks over to the counter and notices the Latina girl staring at him. She's crouched at the wrapping station, where the burgers get packaged and slid out onto the metal chute to be organized into orders, peering over a row of yellow-wrapped Bandito Burritos with eyes as wide and black as tar pits.

She knows.

She saw it, and she served it anyway. Is fully, 100 per cent aware what kind of horror-show she's just pushed through the line to be turned into someone's lunch, someone else's problem. Jesus. What the fuck was she thinking?

Mike answers the question before it's even finished forming in his mind. She's pretty. Pretty Mexican girl. Skin the colour of toasted almond; big, pouty lips; wide, nervous eyes that have probably stared down the business end of a border guard's assault rifle on more than one occasion. Illegal, no doubt. She pukes or screams or breaks down weeping, causes any kind of a scene, the questions start flying, and she's back across the border faster than you can say *ándale arriba*.

He fidgets with his tie again, has to stop himself from chewing on it while he sorts everything out. The tie was a gift from Kara, Egyptian silk.

What if this Mexican chick can't hold it together? What if she wakes up thrashing from a nightmare of bloody digits crawling across her skin like maggots, and spills? Who gets asked questions then?

So, Mike thinks, staring back at her, trying to sound confident in his head—deep-voiced, like Drais. *We find ourselves at a crossroads.* The question is, what's he willing to gamble? What happens if he chucks the thing, wipes it from memory, and she does the same — and he still ends up as a redundancy, a little red mark in the SitcoBVM ledger, just a severance package away from starting over again? Kara's been crystal clear on this point: lose the job, lose her. Lose everything. Become a loser. He's not naive about the allure of his platinum cards.

Fuck it, he thinks in the Drais voice. *You want to get to the top of the food chain, you'd better learn how to chew.*

Mike Stevens, junior VP of marketing for the Pancho's Restaurant Division of SitcoBVM, gives the Mexican girl one last glance, then lifts his eyes up to the bovine face of Vaca Loca on the backlit menu behind the counter and recites in his head, as benediction and penance, the hallowed names of Pancho's trademarked product line: Azteca Burger™, Bandito Burrito™, Torero Chicken™, Taco Fantastico™, Bordertown Chili Fries™, amen. He picks up the sandwich and sinks his teeth down through the whole girth of it as hard as he can, taking a huge bite, snapping through bone, pumping his jaw up and down until the fragment of finger he's torn off has been ground into oblivion, and, making sure she's still watching, swallows with only a barely perceptible flinch. The rest he wraps up and shoves into his satchel, the fate of his career congealing in its blasphemed, mustardy innards. He takes a huge swig of cola and leaves his tray on the table when he gets up to go, a scattering of too-crisp fries cast like divining bones across the translucent paper of the promotional mat.

3. "You're fucking kidding me, right? Fucking *kidding* me."

Carl Drais stares at the soggy pile of dogshit besmirching his oak desk and tries to process the story this lesser minion sitting across from him has just disgorged.

"No sir," says the minion, Mike something-or-other. "No joke, I'm afraid."

"Afraid is the right word, son. Do you have any idea what you're telling me?"

"Yes, sir."

"Do you understand, not just the health code violations that have been perpetrated here, the potential billions in lawsuits, but also how personally fucking disgusted I am at what you've done?"

"I only had the company's best interests in mind, sir."

Carl Drais puts his hands together and leans back in his chair, a move he's practised hundreds of times.

"And I presume you can explain exactly how this particular bit of personal deviance will benefit a multinational conglomerate like SitcoBVM?"

"Well, sir," says minion Mike, "I think it's all a matter of perspective. It was easy to see what a disaster this could turn into for the company —"

"Keen observation!"

"But with a little creativity, it occurred to me that we might be looking at an opportunity here."

Carl frowns, folding his thick brows into an arachnoid ridge. "What I'm looking at is a half-masticated cheeseburger with a fucking zombie finger wedged between the pickles, and a lunatic cannibal shitbag telling me he's eaten half of it in the name of shareholder gains!"

Carl counts out the seconds of silence, watching minion Mike tremble in his chair, smelling the sour sweat leaking from his armpits. He needs the fear. If he doesn't break this man thoroughly — if he lets on too early that he is, in fact, intrigued — things could easily go haywire, as in bankruptcy for the corporation, as in jail time, contraband cigarettes, dropped soap and death by pruno. No idea is anathema to Carl if he can see the money — and there's something here, for sure. Why not? When you know what the fucking beef farms look like, this isn't a stretch at all. It just might be the game-changer. The thing they remember him for. Put his name up there

Between the Pickles

with Ray Kroc and Dave Thomas and the goddamn A&W bear. He has to retain total control, though, complete mastery of the situation, or he runs a major risk of turning into a scapegoat for a board of directors that would charbroil their own mothers to save their hides, if anyone were to find out that Pancho's has been accidentally serving up anonymous human appendages in its Buenos Combos. To work, this has to look intentional.

Eight...nine...ten... Tick-tick. Spidery seconds. He lets them crawl all over minion Mike, get into his ears. Get him primed to do anything Carl wants.

"Now," says Carl. "The first thing is, why should I even believe you? How do I know you're not here to set me up somehow? You come in here making a claim like this, you'd better be ready to back it up without question."

"But the burger, sir—"

"Came out of your cheap man-purse, and could be fake as a silicone tit, for all I know. If I'm inferring correctly, here, it's going to take a more persuasive display of your commitment to the campaign to get me to agree to even poke it with a sterilized ten-foot pole. Brand loyalty starts with the executive, son. You want to sell this thing? You want to convince me it's not just the whim of some deranged pervert? You want to push this kind of radical product on Pancho's ever-fickle customer base? You have to prove to me *you* can love it, first and foremost."

Carl watches minion Mike's face turn pale as bleached flour.

"So," Carl says, leaning in, glancing down at the tepid mass of dry beef, modified corn syrup, wilted vegetables, and human biology nestled in a manger of cheese-caked Pancho's parchment. "Have another bite."

Carl Drais watches his soon-to-be-slightly-less-minor minion absorb the request, digest the inevitable, and steel himself for round two. Truth is, there's so much salt on those goddamn burgers that you could throw a nuclear cow turd on top and most people would never taste the difference. The real challenge will be marketing, and of course convincing the FDA yahoos, but such is the fast food business. That's what Carl Drais has been doing his whole life.

In less than a year, he'll be out, southward bound, blowing his fat retirement package on mojitos and ahi steaks and fishing gear for his Caribbean yacht, *Delilah*. And won't that be grand. Mona yapping in his ear about what a schmuck he is. Floating around the goddamn sea like a sick crustacean, to be gobbled up as chum by bigger, younger fish. Waiting out his palsied years for whatever blood-pressure-related sideswipe to send him plunging over the side of the boat, convulsing, fresh feed for the barracudas. Another stock CEO down; we'll let you know when we put up the memorial plaque next to the shitter and dredge the bones from the ocean floor to cremate and blend into the refried bean mix.

Wouldn't it be great, just once, to really *shake things up?* Do something people will *remember?* Really *change things?* Hasn't he, Carl Drais, earned the right to be something more than just another stray corn kernel passed through the corporate bowel, to be flushed away into obscurity? Truth is, he'd give up every penny in his accounts if he knew it would mean the name Carl Drais made its way into textbooks across the country. Because what good will all the money be, if no one remembers him?

When minion Mike chomps down on the sandwich, looking only slightly paler at actually eating the thing than he did at the suggestion of eating it, Carl knows he's got something he can work with. He watches, silent as a big cat, as Mike chews, his face cycling through the stages of guilt, shame, denial, and acceptance with each roll of the fleshy slurry around his tongue. And when Mike finally swallows, an almost convincing look of greasy satisfaction on his face, Carl smiles.

"Well," he says. "I must say, you look like you quite enjoyed that."

"Yes, sir."

"Listen, Mike—what was your last name again?"

"Stevens, sir."

"Listen, Mike. I must say, on witnessing your unbridled commitment to this new product, I'm warming to it. I'm thinking we may have something here."

Mike Stevens's eyes light up, all the lingering disgust melted away in a ping of hope and newly stoked ambition, and Carl Drais knows that he's got him. Now it's just the final touch, the conspiratorial about-face, and he'll have Stevens ready to eat an entire bucket's worth of deep-fried baby fingers at the flick of his lapel.

"Of course, I'm going to want some time to digest it all. So I'll ask that you leave me now, to see where I can get with it. But, on the way out, you'll want to tell Sheena to order you up some new business cards. If you're going to be handling an account this, let's say, touchy, we'll need you to have access to resources beyond what junior VP clearance allows for." Carl smiles again, spider brows relaxed into a pair of friendly salt-and-pepper caterpillars.

"Yes, sir. Thank you, sir."

"And Mike?"

"Yes sir."

"I'll need you for another meeting tomorrow. After that, you take yourself a bit of a vacation. Maui, or Antigua. Somewhere nice."

"Yes, sir."

When Stevens is gone, Carl Drais picks up the half-eaten sandwich from his desk, a tidbit of finger the length of a thimble still plugged in among the oozing condiments. He waves the burger under his nose, taking in its musk—coaxing, from amid the scents of grease and onion and vinegar, the rarefied aura, the decadent essence that can reveal to him the secret of how to introduce this, his newest baby, to a hungry world.

4. They told her not to worry, but *mierda* is she worried. Worry is a primary ingredient in Rosa's life, but this is worse than the usual kind, the one she gets when burly white men look at her too hard or whenever she passes a policeman on the street. This is sick worry, you-know-what-you-did worry. You-got-yourself-into-some-kind-of-serious-shit worry. You've-been-caught worry. Why else would she be here in the waiting room of SitcoBVM headquarters, told flat out that her presence was not optional? Why else would she be waiting for a meeting with the CEO, a guy she'd never heard of before the company reps showed up at her door telling her that he was "a man of national importance"? Why else would they even have bothered to track down her address, which she's never given the company because her manager pays her under the table in cash? *It's not even a paycheque, Rosa. It's an envelope he hands to you at the end of the week on your way out the door. Paycheques are for real people. Legal people.*

Diego coos and dribbles on her shoulder. She wonders why she bothered putting on the red dress, the only good one she owns, when she knows it's just going to get covered in spit-up. It's bad enough that Valentina's working and she has to carry Diego with her into the lion's den; she had to go and put on lipstick, too. Who gets dressed up to be arrested? But that leads her back to the question that confuses her most, the one that always wedges itself between her and the heavy prison door she keeps imagining swinging in to bang shut over the rest of her life: Why didn't they just send the police to her house? Why bring someone like her into their fancy glass-walled offices?

The receptionist's phone buzzes and she picks it up and nods twice, looking in Rosa's direction, saying "Hmm, yessir." She hangs up and smiles at Rosa.

"Mr. Drais will see you now."

Rosa puts a hand on the back of Diego's little head and stands up. What can she do? Run? Running is what got her here. On shaky legs, she carries her son past the big wooden reception desk that reminds her of a coffin, and walks through the huge doors into the office of Carl Drais, CEO.

"Good afternoon," says the figure standing behind the desk, a tall man with hair like polished grey bone. She looks over into the corner and sees another guy, and when she recognizes him as the one from Pancho's, the one who ate the bad sandwich, she has to blink hard and steady herself to keep from fainting and dropping Diego onto the hardwood.

"Rosa, correct? Rosa Garcia. We've been learning a lot about you."

His smile is a cheese-grater buffed to a perfect shine. The other man sits in the corner, dead still.

"Please don't be alarmed," says Carl Drais in a honey-smoked tone. "Mr. Stevens and I realize what you're probably thinking, but I assure you, we have no intention of reprimanding you, or exploiting your, let us say, documentational circumstances. In fact"—he pauses and comes around the desk, and Rosa reflexively hugs Diego to her chest—"what we'd like to do is offer you an opportunity."

Now his hand is on her shoulder. If he touches Diego, she'll rip at his throat, scratch and bite him bloody, tear him piece by piece until the other one brains her from behind with a paperweight, or just reaches in and touches the barrel of his silenced pistol to her temple to bury a bullet in her skull, like they do in Mafia movies. But Carl Drais's hand stays resting on her upper arm, giving the gentlest squeeze.

"We think you may have, however inadvertently, pointed toward a bold new direction for the Pancho's restaurant chain."

He runs his fingers down her arm to her hand, and he lifts it, his palm cool and dry against her hot, damp one, until it hovers, flat and brown and trembling between them. She's shaking, holding Diego close enough to her that he fuses to her skin, so that there's no way they can tear him from her, with all of it running through her head again: the desert and the dogs and the paycheque and the finger and the night retching in guilt and terror afterward, the men coming to her door, the red dress, the waiting room, and now here, with Carl Drais, which could be worst of all.

"With the right product testing and market research, and of course the small challenge of navigating a few outdated regulations with our friends at the FDA, we believe we might be looking at the next flagship Pancho's sandwich. Still in the earliest stages of development, of course—but for the moment, we're thinking of calling it 'The Dream.' Good, right?"

The one who ate it, Mr. Stevens, stands and walks over to them and looks her in the eyes while he fiddles with his tie. He's younger, and there's something in his own eyes that's not quite fear, not quite nervousness, but a kind of retreat, as though he's pulling back into himself, withdrawing into the flesh and muscle of his big, solid Midwestern body.

"But of course, all of this is only possible with your full cooperation," says Carl Drais. "We can make sure you're well taken care of—take away any question of your right to belong in this nation of ours, give you a permanent position in the company—but you also must understand that the privilege of liberty, so to speak, does not come without a certain sacrifice."

Carl Drais lifts her hand up right close to his face, and for a second she thinks he might kiss her fingers, but he just wafts them under his nose, inhaling deeply.

"So what do you think, Rosa?" he says. "How would you like to be more than just a Wrapper?

Mr. Stevens clears his throat. Diego coughs spittle. Rosa swallows, opens her mouth, blinks. She's remembering the first time she ever ate a Pancho's burger, the day Valentina moved in and they treated themselves to a couple of Pequeño Combos. The way they'd touched their burgers together in a makeshift toast, wrinkled their noses as they chewed the first bites, feeling the salt tingling on their tongues, the limp pickles squeaking between their teeth. How they'd laughed, almost rejoicing in the luxury of throwing away half their lunches. Shaking their heads, saying, what a country. What a country, this.

The
Last Ham

He was a colourful character who was not accepted by the establishment because he fought against privilege and for the little guy. My plan is to be more successful than he was.

—Rob Ford

1. The pig carcass hung from a thick wooden beam, spinning at the end of a rope trussed around its trotters, shafts of light from the gaps in the barn walls dancing like cracked player piano keys across its pale, hairless girth. A tendril of blood drizzled from the slice in its neck into the bucket underneath, pushing yet more blood over the bucket's rim into a pool on the dirt floor that now framed the crumpled body of Ted Kersey like a scarlet peacock's fan. As a whole, the tableau suggested some obscene ritual sacrifice, the work of a brutal priest who placed the same value on the souls of men as on those of swine for the butchering.

This was what Helen Kersey found when she walked into the barn to tell Ted she was back from the grocery store and that dinner would be ready in twenty minutes, and given the nature of the scene, it's hardly surprising that her first instinct was not to call an ambulance, but to run into the house and telephone Sister Mary Beth Boultbee of St. Ignatius Catholic Church to ask her, between choking sobs, what sort of God would allow this kind of indignity to happen to a decent man.

"The Lord's plan has some strange twists and turns," said the Sister. "But we must have faith in His word and His wisdom, cruel though it may seem."

Questions hovered around Ted Kersey's death like scavenging gulls. There were the clinical facts: Ted had died of a massive cardiac event that occurred while he was slaughtering the fattest hog of the season for Bedford's Annual Easter Picnic and Church Auction. The hospital records listed him as DOA, official pronouncement at 7:32 p.m. Most everything else to do with the incident was subject to controversy. Speculation ran from the practical to the occult. Had the attack been brought on by the physical strain of killing the pig? Was this usually a job Ted did alone, or had queer circumstances left him without assistance? Did he die in tandem with the beast, as he ran the blade across its throat? Or had the attack come moments later, triggered by the release of the animal's blood, as though it had poisoned the very air Ted breathed? Had the pig been possessed by some demonic spirit? Why had this blasphemy happened to Ted Kersey? Why now?

After being bandied about in church and on the walkways of Bedford's tiny main street for a few days, most of these questions were shrugged off as mysteries beyond the ken of the town's average folk. "God knows the answers, and that's enough," said Sister Mary Beth, when a reporter from the *Dufferin Free Muskrat* asked her whether or not this turn of events would cast a pall over the beloved annual picnic.

Yet there were questions that refused to go away, and it was these that came to taint the air of Dufferin County for a few strange weeks with the delirious haze of a high fever and the queasy stink of rotten meat.

Ted Kersey had provided the St. Ignatius Easter Auction with a ham for thirty-three years running. Over time, it had become the centrepiece of the auction, a coveted prize that won Ted a reputation as the best hog farmer in the county, and fetched large sums that Sister Mary Beth relied on for the annual spring cleaning at the parish. But the macabre pedigree of this year's ham made people nervous. In the days following Ted Kersey's death, Sister Mary Beth had to field many questions from worried members of the congregation.

"Is the meat cursed?"

"Would it be sacrilege to eat such a thing?"

"Will the ham appear at the auction at all?"

These concerns and others would have been much simpler to assuage if not for the actions of Dale Westin.

On the night Ted died, after Sister Mary Beth hung up the phone on a wailing Helen Kersey, she called an ambulance, then immediately went to find Jeff Stooley, the church handyman. The Sister was as pragmatic as she was compassionate, and she hoped that while she calmed Helen by telling her that surely Ted's years of service to the church would win him a prime seat in heaven, Jeff could clean up the blood and cart away the pig carcass, ostensibly to save Helen the trauma of doing it, but also to save the auction's most lucrative item from turning into a feast for flies and marauding raccoons.

"I want you to take the ham straight to Girardi's," the Sister said, wagging her wimple in her bobble-headed yet no-nonsense way. The Sister intended to have Gerry Girardi, a regular reader at Sunday service and proprietor of the town's oldest butcher shop, clean, eviscerate, and carve up the animal, making sure to take special care with the ham — which, based on what she had gleaned from her few visits to the Kersey farm over the past year, was an exceptional specimen, as fat and succulent a hog's leg as had ever appeared in the service of the Lord and his small but devoted flock at St. Ignatius. Ted Kersey would be thanked for giving his life to the service of the Lord, and a plaque would be erected in his honour beside the geraniums in the church garden.

Dale Westin had a different idea. Dale was a wealthy former CEO from the city, who'd taken early retirement and moved out to Dufferin County to spend his golden years playing golf and shooting game birds on the fifty-five acres out back of the rustic sports lodge he'd had built just down the road from the Kersey farm. He told everyone who would listen how much he loved the country air. "Good, honest air you got up here," he'd say. But some knew there was something off about Dale Westin from the start. Within weeks of moving in, he became notorious for a habit of keeping close tabs on the personal affairs of everyone in town, ostensibly in the spirit of neighbourly goodwill, but in fact, some said, because he needed an excuse to create spreadsheets now that his high-finance days were behind him.

Outside of his public exaltations, Dale Westin kept a tight lid on his own affairs, so there was no knowing exactly what went through his head as he looked out his window on that cool March evening and saw the ambulance parked out at the Kersey place. Just as Sister Mary Beth knew how to approach a situation from several different angles at once, Dale Westin had his own nose for finding opportunity where others saw merely offal, and whether it was divine inspiration or something more calculated, he took it upon himself to make the tragedy at the neighbouring farm his business. When he pulled his Range Rover into the Kerseys' driveway that night, wearing the red-and-black checkered lumberjack coat he'd purchased to blend in with the locals, he nearly rear-ended Jeff Stooley's pickup as it was backing out, headed for Girardi's, the pig carcass prone and reeking and lashed to the truck bed with bloodied twine.

"Call me a jumper to conclusions, Jeff," Dale Westin said as he hopped out of the Rover and went up to lean into the truck's driver-side window before Jeff Stooley even had a chance to roll it down fully, "but it seems to me like there might be some kind of situation going on here that could require a little help. Jeff, I know you know that I value the well-being of every man and woman in this community, so I thought I'd come on by and see if I could lend a hand with anything that needs doing. Whatcha got there?" He waved his thumb at the truck bed, seeing full well for himself that there was a dead hog in it.

Jeff Stooley hesitated for a moment, but he was no match for Dale Westin's polished-dime smile. "Uh, got Ted Kersey's picnic pig," said Jeff, leaning out the window of the idling truck. "I gotta take it down to Gerry Girardi to make sure it gets stored right for the auction."

"What's with the ambulance?" said Dale, breath billowing steam out in the crisp air. "A neighbour's concerned, you know. Has there been an injury?"

"Teddy's bit the dust," said Jeff, a note of bewilderment in his voice, as though he'd only just considered the truth of the situation.

"You mean he's dead?" said Dale Westin.

"That's right," said Jeff. "Keeled over in the act of slaughterin' this pig. Sister Mary Beth's down there consoling his wife."

"God, that's horrible!" said Dale Westin, removing his gloves. "Tragic. Poor Helen! I only knew Ted for a short period, but he was a stand-up guy and a damn good farmer, and of course I've heard nothing but raves about his pork."

"Well, this fellow here will probably be the last of it," said Jeff, waving a thumb at the pig carcass. "Ted's got no kids, and I don't rightly see Helen having it in her to keep the farm goin' by herself."

"The last ham?" said Dale. "It can't be the last ham! The Easter ham is a Dufferin County tradition, Jeff! It's part of what makes this community great."

"Be honest with you, I never tasted any of Ted's hams," said Jeff. "Too dear for my blood, and I serve the church in other ways."

"Well, I've never tasted one either, but I know them by reputation," Dale said. "You come here as a keen observer, it's pretty darned clear what the annual ham means to the good folks who live and die tilling this ground. As a humble citizen who is proud of what this county has to offer, and sees real quality in the way it upholds its values and understands the good things in life, I'm inclined to take it on myself to see to it that this ham gets the treatment it deserves."

"I think Sister Mary Beth's on top of that," said Jeff, sensing some threat that he could not quite place. "Gerry Girardi's been butcherin' the Easter ham for years, and I expect he'll give this one extra-special attention, under the circumstances."

"Gerry Girardi is a fine fellow," said Dale Westin. "Yvette cooked me up one of his chops just last night, and I'll be damned if it wasn't delicious. But this hog is not destined for the same old same old. This hog is *singular*. Why don't you drive it on over to my place, and I'll make the appropriate arrangements. We're gonna have us an exceptional ham this year, in the name of Ted Kersey, God rest his soul."

"Well," said Jeff, "I'd better ask Sister Mary Beth."

"Look, Sister Mary Beth will tell you that Dale Westin put a hundred bucks in the collection plate last time he was at Mass, so she knows Dale Westin has the town's best interests in mind. It's what the people of Bedford would want, Jeff. I don't think you're the type to want to stand in the way of that, are you?"

Jeff looked worried, but he was the sort to respect men like Dale Westin, who talked as though he was addressing a roomful of important people even when it was just the plain old church handyman he was talking to. Jeff eyed the carcass. He eyed the Range Rover, which was still blocking his pickup. He eyed Dale Westin, who was standing there staring at him with a grin wide and sharp enough to thresh wheat.

"You just follow the Rover," Dale said, not moving.

"You're gonna have to explain this to Sister Mary Beth," said Jeff.

"You don't have anything to worry about," said Dale. "I have your back. I'm for the people."

2. Although Jeff Stooley retained his job at the church, it was said that his penance for handing the ham over to Dale Westin involved several thousand Hail Marys, a week of hard work cleaning out the church's clogged eaves, and a tongue-lashing from the Sister that would have made Lucifer himself blush. But she saved her worst words for Dale Westin. Sister Mary Beth publicly refused to repeat the telephone conversation she'd had with Westin about what she termed "the abduction," but her subsequent call to the police and statements to the newspaper made her position clear: the interception of the St. Ignatius pig carcass was theft of church property, a slap in the face to God, and a reprehensible response to a deep and genuine tragedy. She intended to pursue every possible course of action to see Dale Westin punished for his outsider's indifference to the laws and customs that had always served the good, pious people of Dufferin County.

The police agreed to question Dale, but ultimately no charges were pressed.

Sheriff John Bays Jr., a Presbyterian who had been invited to shoot geese on Dale Westin's back lot on more than one occasion, declared that the hog carcass had never been officially donated to the church and could therefore not be said to have been stolen, and that if anything it belonged to Helen Kersey, who, the day after Ted's funeral, had flown to Los Angeles to spend an extended sojourn with her sister and whom no one had been able to reach since. And so it was that Sheriff Bays decided, until further notice and given the perishable nature of the item in question, that until the time of auction, the contested carcass would remain in the custody of Dale Westin, whose own statements to the police and newspapers maintained that he was only trying to do right by the taxpaying citizens of the county by preserving one of its most sacred annual events. It was no secret that, even as he was making these statements, Dale Westin had already been in contact with a butcher from the city about coming up to carve the hog and cure the ham (and almost certainly, the town gossips said in scandalized tones, to spend a day or two hunting ducks out back the lodge and having the woman called Yvette cook them up in a foreign style).

"Ladies and gentlemen, a scourge has come upon our town!" This was how Father Angus Merriweather, drunker than usual, began his sermon that Sunday, a particularly vitriolic screed about the evils of money and presumption that Sister Mary Beth Boultbee sat through with hands clasped tightly in her lap, murmuring what were either prayers or curses; the pinched look on her face gave no indication which. Dale Westin was notably absent from the congregation. Sister Mary Beth had put his donated hundred-dollar bill in an envelope and told Jeff Stooley to drive out and put it in his mailbox with a card, printed with an image of a burning heart and a quote from Psalms, "Therefore the wicked will not stand in the judgment, nor sinners in the congregation of the righteous," so no one was surprised when he didn't show up. A few old-timers milling around in the vestibule after Mass even speculated that, were Dale Westin to cross the threshold of St. Ignatius just now, it would cause either his own body or the church spire to erupt spontaneously into cold blue flame.

It wasn't long before the gossip evolved into more toxic rhetoric. Anxiety seeped into the town's soil like a chemical spill. Days after the sermon, the first letters sprang up in the *Free Muskrat*, turning the ham into a full-blown issue of public concern. The accusations were made with Biblical intensity: Dale Westin was a Satan from the city here to sabotage the town's most beloved annual event. His business and political affairs had ended in disaster down south, so he'd come to Dufferin County to wreak havoc on its overly trusting, God-fearing people. He was a thief and a philistine, a shyster and an elitist, and, according to one especially intense letter, probably a pederast. Seven separate letters constituting a whole page were published, each demanding the immediate return of the ham to the church, one calling for the arrest and castration of Dale Westin, and one going so far as to suggest he'd engineered the murder of Ted Kersey so as to be able to take possession of the ham for use in some kind of disgusting pagan ceremony. A strange follow-up letter, published two days later and signed Anonymous, claimed that the ham contained Ted Kersey's earthbound soul, and that its capture amounted to an act of spiritual torture that would only be forgiven when it was placed upon the auction block and all was made right in the world again. Another anonymous letter appeared in the weekend edition, ostensibly staying neutral in matters of politics or faith but implicitly responding to the earlier claim about Ted Kersey's trapped soul, condemning the association of the imperfections of the physical realm with the finer qualities of the spirit, and asking why God would trap Ted Kersey's ghost in a ham or the soul of Our Lady of Lourdes in a plain old tomato, anyhow.

Amid the accusations and uncertainties, one hard fact began to assert itself: with speculation at destabilizing levels, the ham would have to be revealed to a public starving for a sneak peek. Anticipation grew by the day. The main street of Bedford, which moved at the pace of a sun-drunk mule in summer and was swallowed by shadows and snow in the long winter, began to buzz with the tension of a city on the edge of great change. Every conversation in the town danced cautiously around the subject of the ham, and the mention of Dale Westin's name was said to have set off a fight at McNulty's Bar that got particularly violent, a window smashed out, blood on the sidewalk. The April thaw sent dirty water sluicing down the curbsides, and everyone stepped carefully, to avoid not just the slushy runoff but also the threat of being pulled down into the general argument, a tangle of wet, frayed anger growling in the gutter that could grab them at any time. Girardi's temporarily suspended the sale of all ham products, fearing that the release of such contentious meat into the general gnashing might tip the town into flat-out chaos. Mayor Terry McMurrich made a plea for calm in the *Free Muskrat*, and Father Merriweather's drinking became so bad that he showed up late for Mass and botched the words to the doxology. Of Sister Mary Beth Boultbee, no one heard a thing; the nun had locked herself in the convent behind St. Ignatius, emerging only to sit at the back left of the altar at Sunday service, her face hidden under a dusky black veil, the very image of mourning.

During this time, the collective energy of the town underwent an unmistakable shift, condensing and focusing like a spotlight on the lodge up by the Kersey farm, where Dale Westin had retreated into fortified silence. For days, nothing but the regular salvo of early-evening gunfire was heard from his property. The lack of communication on the status of the captive ham made the towns-people's imaginations run wild, and rumours began circulating, saying it was being defiled, who-knows-what being done to it by the butcher from the city, some foreign glaze of flamboyant curing process, a trap set by Mammon, recipe as hex. The air in Bedford seemed on the verge of rupture.

Then, one day in early April, under the broad spring sunshine, Dale Westin's black Range Rover pulled onto Main Street and rolled into the middle of town, as brash and surreal a sight as if the corpse of Ted Kersey himself had climbed out of the grave and lumbered into the drugstore to tell them there was something wonky with his heart. All along the street, eyes peered from behind windows, locked on Dale Westin as he steered the vehicle up to the church, emerged from the driver's seat, and went around the back to pull from the trunk a wheeled dolly and a massive cloaked thing, which he placed on the dolly and rolled in through the front doors of St. Ignatius Catholic Church as though he'd dug up the skull of John the Baptist from the earth below Damascus and was now hauling it up to the altar to lay at the feet of Sister Mary Beth Boultbee, a gesture of deep penitence or gross blasphemy, or both. Safe in their homes, which many people had begun locking since the start of the queer happenings, no one spoke above a whisper.

The church doors stayed closed through the day and night. By dawn, Father Merriweather, who had fled the scene in chicken-heartedness, choosing a blind bender through the nighttime streets over a willing role in whatever Black Mass was unfolding within the seat of his debauched curacy, was drunk enough to go up to the doors and splay his hands before them, feeling for seismic vibration. But he would not dare touch his skin to their pressurized surface. It was seven a.m. by the time the phones rang in the kitchens of several key members of the church congregation, who in turn spread the news to their neighbours, local shopkeepers, the cottage country radio station, the *Free Muskrat*, and the city newspapermen from the

Star and the *Sun* who had taken rooms at the Bedford Inn: that day, at the stroke of noon, on the steps of St. Ignatius Catholic Church, with the plain light of midday and God as a witness, there would be a public announcement regarding the Annual Easter Picnic and Church Auction and the fate of the now-infamous Kersey Ham.

As the hour approached, a crowd of over a hundred gathered outside the church. There were middle-aged farmers with sunbaked faces and suspicious eyes, teens trying hard not to look as curious as they actually were, and old-timers looking as though they disapproved of the whole scene. There was Buck Henry from the *Free Muskrat* with his beat-up yellow notepad, newspapermen from nearby towns with their Dictaphones and cameras, and television trucks from the city bearing shellac-haired news reporters with logoed microphones. Sheriff John Bays Jr. had his two best men flanking the church steps, at the base of which someone had, for whatever reason, laid a bouquet of perfect white roses.

The second that the clock on City Hall across the square from the church ticked over to noon, a great clanging exploded out from the belfry, sending a wave of anxious muttering through the crowd. The doors cracked open, causing a collective inhalation, and the air seemed to thicken so that the entire scene appeared to those watching from afar to congeal into a wax display on the church lawn, stilled congregants awaiting their rapture: either blinding gold entry into the kingdom of piety and tradition, or the sentence of cold, hamless darkness.

The doors now parted, the stone rolled away, and into this electricity emerged the largest, pinkest piece of meat anyone in attendance had ever seen — a perfectly shaped leg with the girth of a beer barrel, tapering down honey-glazed skin to a polished white bone, pushing before it a haze of air kissed with smoke, rosemary, orange peel, and a hint of cloves, which made several photographers shoved up close to the doors swoon backwards, overwhelmed by the intense deliciousness of the aroma, their photos blurred forever by the ham's sheer karmic presence. Following the ham out of the gloom were Dale Westin, beaming like a white shark, and Sister Mary Beth Boultbee, her cowl rumpled and her face drooping and her eyes as stormy and dark as a thundercloud. The photographers scrambled to regroup, firing off flashes to capture the moment when the ham, and Dale Westin, truly began to follow their strange conjoined destiny.

"Greetings, fellow citizens of Bedford, in beautiful Dufferin County!" said Dale Westin, waving his arm out across the crowd with a majestic sweep. "I am more pleased than you can know to be here today to make the announcement that I know you have all been waiting for." The noon sunlight glinted off Dale Westin's forehead, as smooth and shiny as a maraschino cherry. "Myself and Sister Mary Beth Boultbee have been having an invigorating round of discussions. It has not been an easy road. But I think you will all agree that, after careful consideration, we've decided on what is best for the people of this town." Dale Westin's pause here could have felled a horse, and in fact someone in the audience fainted. "Next Sunday, when the St. Ignatius Annual Easter Picnic Auction gets underway, this magnificent specimen, provided to the town by the dear departed Mr. Theodore Kersey, God rest his soul, will be *up on the auction block for all to bid on, as befits the proud tradition of this town!*"

A warped cheer went up from the crowd. Cameras rolled on the scene: people clapped and whistled, others booed and hissed, some unfurled homemade banners supporting the church or the ham or both, or simply wishing everyone Happy Easter. Dale Westin, who was standing behind the ham as though it were a podium, raised his hand over it to call for silence and thus appeared to be extracting from it some kind of invisible energy comparable to that said to emanate from volcanic rock or crystals. The din lowered with his hand.

"Thank you," he said. "I know Sister Mary Beth and I are both very pleased that this has worked out the way it has." Behind him, Sister Mary Beth glowered, her eyes hardened into cold black flint. "The St. Ignatius Annual Easter Picnic and Church Auction embodies the qualities that make Bedford the strong, principled, and beautiful community it is. They're the same qualities that Ted Kersey embraced in his farming, the same qualities you all embrace in your efforts to make the community a great place to live. Folks, it's these same qualities that I, Dale Westin, have been observing and falling in love with since I arrived in Dufferin County. *And so.*" Here Dale Westin paused yet again, his face ruddy in the reflected light bouncing up off the ham's honey-dark rind, his eyes scanning the crowd with concentrated verve. "*And so*, it is with great pride that I take this opportunity not only to bring you good tidings about the auction and the ham, but also to announce to you, the good people of Bedford, my candidacy for mayor in the coming election!"

The tumult that followed this statement is now officially considered to be the first of the Bedford Ham Riots. Upon announcing his intention to run for municipal office, Dale Westin was greeted with a chorus of sounds so ugly and incomprehensible in its emotional bent that those who heard it swear it made the spires of St. Ignatius droop. Sister Mary Beth Boultbee, already dying from humiliation but now pushed to the edge of nervous breakdown by the long collective dissonance, summoned Jeff Stooley from inside the church and had him roll the Kersey Ham back into the safety of the Lord's house. This proved a wise decision when, mere minutes later, a masked figure emerged from the crowd, ran up the first three steps of St. Ignatius, and hurled a bucket of pig's blood all over Dale Westin, who reeled backward and nearly elbowed Sister Mary Beth in the eye before he regained his footing and, dripping with blood, yelled into the crowd, now a roiling hive of curses, clothes-grabbing, sign-waving, and general skirmish, "*Dale Westin, for the people of*

Dufferin County! Dale Westin has brought your ham back to you! Elect Dale Westin!"

It took provincial officers half an hour to arrive on the scene, where they found the square in front of the church littered with torn cardboard, tufts of hair, several dozen rioters, and both of the town's police lieutenants (Sheriff Bays nowhere to be found), all of whom had met the wrong end of a foot, fist, or blunt object and were now rolling around, holding their injured parts and wailing. The closest hospital, thirty minutes away in Orangeville, had to set up cots in the hallways to accommodate the injured. A stone gargoyle on the facade of St. Ignatius had been lopped off and apparently used as a weapon. From that night on, police walked the streets of Bedford around the clock, radios cackling on their belts and glossy black batons swinging at their hips. The doors of St. Ignatius were guarded by two officers with accompanying German shepherds, to prevent violence but also to keep the new surge of nosy city reporters, who had caught the scent of blood in the riots, from turning the church into a film set. Mayor McMurrich issued a statement condemning the destruction and reminding the town's citizens of the years of loyal service he'd provided them, including a list of all the various fixes, improvements, and blessings he'd bestowed on local businesses during his tenure.

And up the road, next to the darkened Kersey farm, a massive iron fence topped with closed-circuit cameras (beamed, they said, straight into the office of Sheriff John Bays Jr.) appeared overnight around the Westin lodge, warning anyone who approached that Dale Westin was now to be considered a town VIP, and as such would not tolerate intruders kindly.

3. "Before we begin the bidding, I would ask that we all take a moment to remember Ted Kersey, who gave his life so that this fine specimen could be shared with all of you ... Before we begin the bidding, I would ask... Before the bidding, I would like to take a moment..."

Dale Westin faced the full-length mirror, dressed in a suit of fine black silk. He smelled of musk and woodsmoke. His hair was greased to a slick shine where it came to a point on his forehead. The glow of the dimmed pot lights shimmered off the gilt mirror frame and gave his face the brassy orange cast of an Egyptian mask, and when he smiled, his teeth blazed out with the paralyzing blue-white light of a laser beam. The room was bare except for the mirror and a desk in the shadows, and his face hovered in the gloam, a ghostly disc of light, like the halo cast by a huge votive candle burning in an empty chapel otherwise stripped of devotional ornament.

"Great deeds require great sacrifice," he said. "Before we begin the bidding, I would like to take a moment to remember the man who gave his life for this."

Dale Westin adjusted his powder-blue tie and turned to walk over to the window. The moon was shining over the wooded hills, tinting the view with inky indigos and pale greys. There was still some ice clinging to the pines, and the air was cold and clear, making the lines of the landscape stand out with the precision of a steel etching. No one would say it was not a perfect night in Dufferin County.

In a copse of trees not far from the window, the yellow-green eyes of a whitetail doe flashed out in the darkness. It was standing just behind a small fir, looking toward the house, silent and still. Dale could see it in the moonlight, outlined against the sky, eyes round and shining like doubloons. He walked over to the desk, snatched one last shred of meat from a plate holding the ravaged carcass of a roast duck, and picked up the long black hunting rifle lying beside it. The sound of the bolt action was dry and compressed in the warm air of the room. There was no wind as Dale opened the door onto the ghostly world of the moonlit back acres of his property, and the deer did not seem to notice him as he walked straight out into the night toward its silhouetted form, stopped six feet away to raise the stock to his shoulder, took sight, and shot it through the right eye, the crack echoing out through the night like a gavel over heaven. Blood sprayed from the deer's face as it fell, its intact eye fading to the dull sheen of a dead fish as its routed head smacked into the mushy ground. Dale walked over and put his hand on the animal's neck and over the soft fuzz covering its nose to make sure it had stopped breathing. Its blood oozed into a puddle around his shoe, vivid red at first, then fading to black as it seeped into the shadowed earth, its colour leaching away with its vitality. He waited until he felt the warmth go out of the deer, got up and turned, and walked back into the lodge, shutting the door behind him, the land gleaming like cold blue stone in the country night.

4. The day broke on what at first glance anyone would have told you was a lovely morning in Dufferin County, quiet streets streaked with yellow and pink, the dewy haze casting the scene in the softened lines and melancholy light of an Impressionist painting. As the shadows receded from under the awnings and eaves of sleepy Bedford, the birds chirping their springtime return, the weight of human affairs not yet settled on the day, there was a palpable moment in which the tension that had choked the town since the death of Ted Kersey slackened away in the utter normalcy of the season turning over in the breeze. Sensible calm lay over Bedford and its outlying farmland like a spectral hand conferring a whispered blessing—even up at the Westin lodge, where a murder of crows had been circling the air over the wooded back slopes since before dawn.

It was in the centre of town that the first fissure appeared in dawn-time Bedford's luminous, postcard-worthy gloss of tranquility. It came in the form of a dark figure, just a silhouette at first, seeming to hover out from the stout white-brick facade of the old county courthouse across the square from St. Ignatius. Slowly, the bulbous middle and lumpen top emerged in shades of dark khaki and burlap tan as the unmistakable gut and Stetson of Sheriff John Bays Jr., swinging his rigid black truncheon in a slow circle at his side. By the time the first rooster crowed out across the ploughed fields, the sheriff had already taken position on the steps of the little white gazebo in the middle of the square—where, in a matter of hours, the Kersey Ham would be rolled out and placed on a stone plinth serving as an auction block, offering whoever was brave or foolhardy enough to try and possess such a thing the chance to gaze on it and pledge a dollar-value worthy of its outsized legend.

The march of John Bays Jr. into the square was the first trickle of human presence in what was soon a veritable deluge. Not five minutes after the sheriff had set his haunches in a stout squat on the white wooden steps, his hand resting on the butt of his handgun, other dark figures began to flow out from the seams of the waking town, first a few lone wanderers, then huddled pairs, then groups of three and four, and finally a ceaseless and unbroken flow of people, more than the town had ever seen before, hundreds swarming out like ants and coming to surround the gazebo in a dense sphincter of humanity that pulsed in waves of tense, oily anticipation.

By the time the morning sun pulled its way up over the church steeple and the bells of St. Ignatius rang out to mark seven o'clock, the square was a solid mass, humming with chatter and barely contained agitation. Phineas "Old Pa" Deasey, said to be the oldest person in town by at least a decade, had been rolled up to the roof of the post office by request in order to witness the auction from a strategic but safe position, and, looking down on the growing multitude, declared to the sky that this gathering of souls hungry for a meal of cursed ham was the queerest and most disturbing sight ever to manifest itself within the borders of Dufferin County, and he included in this the death of his eldest son by runaway tractor and the time a rabid moose ran amok through Henderson's Drugs in the broad light of day. The auction was scheduled to begin at nine a.m. sharp, and by eight thirty Old Pa had already finished half the bottle of Wild Turkey he'd brought up to the roof to console himself with while things went all to hell down below.

At nine o'clock, once again accompanied by the clanging of bells, came the most awkward event of the morning, the one that made many in the crowd squirm with pangs of latent guilt: the emergence, from the same church that had not one week prior disgorged Dale Westin and his surprise campaign promise, of Sister Mary Beth Boultbee. Her wimpled head was crooked forward with deeply root-ed condemnation as she strode toward the gazebo to announce the beginning of the event, usually such a joyous occasion in the year, but now besmirched in her mind to the point of calamity. Sensing on the Sister the rage of the vengeful and lunatic God of Revelation, the tightly squished crowd somehow found the room and will to spread out before her, cleaving a path in the crush of skin and bones and hair and sweat, and falling silent as she ascended the white steps of the gazebo, casting a glance at Sheriff John Bays Jr. that could have rent and tanned the skin from a whole herd of cattle in half a second. Wrathful and silent, the Sister took her place behind the podium set up beside the empty plinth waiting to be crowned by the massive piece of pork that had attained both the significance of a holy artifact and the blasphemy of a debased relic, the Hope Diamond swaddled in the Shroud of Turin, the heart of Christ wrapped in bacon and cured to withstand the appetites of the eons.

The microphone whined as the Sister finally leaned forward and began to speak.

"Good people of Bedford, Dufferin County, and beyond," said Sister Mary Beth, her voice flat, save for a trembling around the edges. "I thank you all for coming, although I would be lying in full view of the Lord our Saviour Jesus Christ if I did not admit that it is with some hesitation that I welcome you to the thirty-ninth annual St. Ignatius Easter Picnic Auction."

The crowd convulsed in response, and the strangled, backfiring sound that issued from its thousand mouths was equal parts elation, terror, relief, blood lust, disapproval, and paralyzing stupefaction. It settled as abruptly and violently as it had begun, and Sister Mary Beth continued.

"I know that you are all here for one reason, and one reason alone, which has grown in infamy such that I need not speak its name until the time is come for it to be borne up onto its pedestal to face the eyes of God and all of you. HOWEVER." From where Sister Mary Beth stood on the gazebo, the air above the crowd appeared to shimmer with the distorting heat of a flame-kissed grill. "I implore you at this time to let the auction proceed as scheduled, to follow the auctioning of lots as it has been laid out in the program so kindly provided to us by Alice Cahill and the good folks who run the copy machine at Henderson's Drugs." Sister Mary Beth danced her careful, precarious waltz with normalcy, struggling in the only way she had left to bring the auction back down to the sane and sanctified earth. "We have many lovely items, donated by members of the community to help raise funds for the parish—"

"*Bring us the ham!*"

This shout was clear and inflamed with rage, although its origin was impossible to pinpoint, as within seconds it was being echoed throughout the crowd, a rising wave of voices that took almost no time to move up through the registers of gabble and cacophony to cohere into a vicious chant:

"*BRING THE HAM! BRING THE HAM! BRING THE HAM! BRING THE HAM!*"

Sister Mary Beth's shoulders slumped, and it is said that her face aged decades in a matter of seconds, the lines of defeat and death creeping out like cracks on a windshield from the corners of her eyes and lips. She held up her hand and the crowd's clamour settled into the mild hissing of a nest of snakes. Glowering at them with hate-seared eyes, the Sister said, simply, "Let it be so."

A maniacal, snarling cheer erupted among the congregants and echoed off the buildings and scraped the sky above Bedford with its unholy roar. What happened next is considered to be the moment at which the Second Bedford Ham Riot became inevitable. There is not a soul who has been asked (and many have) who can verify for certain when or how or whence the figure of Dale Westin, dressed in a white suit that beamed like polished ivory, appeared amid the crowd, holding aloft, in a feat of flabbergasting strength, the Kersey Ham: an object of near-solar radiance and power and scrumptiousness, an idol to end all idols, not merely a ham any longer, in any normal sense of the word, so much as an ark within which the secrets of the universe were believed by most everyone who stared upon it that day to be contained. Dale Westin, Atlas of the Ham, having suddenly materialized in the middle of a crowd of thousands, seemed to float toward the gazebo, his face incarnadine, his smile as wide and toothy as the great curving colonnades of St. Peter's Square. When he finally set foot on the first step, nodding a happy salutation to Sheriff Bays and pointedly ignoring the soot-black stare of the Sister, the structure creaked under his weight—and then, slowly but discernibly, the meat he held began to hum, a low-frequency choral sound that contained within its registers both the sanctity of vespers floating upward into the dome of a grand cathedral, and the volatility of uranium on the verge of exploding into nuclear immolation. The people were afraid; the people were ecstatic. Flexing his arms in a gesture of elation and strength, Dale Westin lifted the Kersey Ham once, twice, and three times, and then brought it down to rest on the plinth with all the reverence and care one might take in laying a newborn babe in its cradle for the first time. He turned to the crowd, spread his arms out wide, brought them in like folding wings to his face, touched the palms of his hands to his lips, made an unctuous smacking sound, and spread his arms out wide again, showering the aura of blessed ham over the congregants, rapturously unaware of the faint odour of carrion wafting out on the breath of his flourish.

"Good morning, folks! Great deeds require great sacrifice. Before we begin the bidding," he said into the microphone from which Sister Mary Beth Boultbee had retreated to hide in the shadow of the gazebo's roof, covering her nose with her habit. "I would ask that we all take a moment to remember the man who gave his life so that this magnificent specimen you see before you could be cut, cured, and finished, under the expert supervision of the finest butcher in the country, and be brought here today to amaze, delight, and edify the good people of Dufferin County, such that this wonderful tradition, a true symbol of this town's solid, earthy heart, could be upheld!"

From somewhere in the middle of the crowd, a voice shot up like a geyser, impatient, fevered, hungry: "A THOUSAND DOLLARS!"

"TWO THOUSAND!" came a faceless reply.

"Good people," said Dale Westin, "let's take a moment to—"

"FIVE THOUSAND DOLLARS!"

"TEN!"

"TWELVE!"

"TWENTY-FIVE THOUSAND DOLLARS!"

"THE HAM FOR MAYOR!"

"THE HAM IS THE ANTICHRIST!"

For a moment, it looked as though things were about to spin out of control, the bids coming fast, crazed, from all directions, order slowly beginning to dissolve in a squirming ataxia of desire. But then, at a crucial moment, just as the bellowing of ever-larger sums threatened to become incoherent, one cry rose up above all else to pierce through the white noise like a rusty nail speared through an overstuffed sausage. Bidders and watchers and objectors and worshippers alike turned to see, fighting his way through the crowd with zombie resolution and holding aloft some blackened, sinewed trophy of his own, the lurching form and burning eyes of Jeff Stooley, the church caretaker. As they had done with Sister Boultbee, as they had done with Dale Westin and the ham, the crowd once again parted to let this madness pass through them and make its way to the gazebo, where Dale Westin stood, awestruck.

"Why, Jeff," he said, seeming completely at a loss as to how to receive this man who had helped him procure the ham but was clearly too ignorant to be affected by its charms. "What have you got there?"

At this, Jeff Stooley, ravaged by guilt and shame and rye whiskey, tossed his prize up onto the platform, arcing it through the air like a sack of gold pillaged from a treasure hoard. As the sun shone on its mottled form, those near the front of the crowd recognized it—although only one woman, whose name is unknown, was able to fight through the revulsion that had welled up in her chest like molten fire to scream out and let the world know what Jeff Stooley had chucked up to a rolling stop at the base of the plinth that held the infamous pink supper.

"Good Lord Jesus!" she cried. *"It's the head of Ted Kersey himself!"*

And so it was—the nose pushed in and trailing skeins of rotten flesh, the hair bristling like barbed wire, the eye sockets hollow black pits that stared up at Dale Westin with naked recognition, saying in silent doom, *I can see you.* With that one first scream now avalanching into a raving, deafening, uncontrolled thrum of terror and frenzy all around him, Dale Westin looked deep into the dismembered head's cavernous gaze, and smiled.

Newspaper reports of the subsequent incident variously focused on the arrest of Jeff Stooley, the culpability of the Church, or the overriding grotesquerie of the event. Its central totems and mysteries were buffered to the point of inconsequence by various sidebars, personal accounts, editorials, and outright fictions. Video footage of the grim hours following the unceremonious deposit of Ted Kersey's head at the foot of the gazebo focused almost exclusively on the different acts of violence that the crowd thus began inflicting on one another, the final release of accumulated tension that had been haunting these normally placid and contented folk for the duration of a blighted Easter season. One cameraman managed to capture Sister Mary Beth Boultbee casting her wimple aside and clawing her way down the steps of the gazebo, heading with holy fury toward the doors of St. Ignatius. Later, when the Sister was interviewed on camera, she had precious little to say beyond announcing that she intended to request a relocation to someplace where people still feared the Lord and lived sane and wholesome lives.

Of course, the most analyzed and debated and frequently viewed piece of footage, captured by a cameraman from a downtown news channel, was the one tiny segment that gave the only hint of what might have actually happened — never verifiable due to a vantage point that was obscured by a stray foot, or a storm of fists, or a body lurching into the frame — the atrocity that many believe to have occurred, but which not a single soul in or within a hundred kilometres of Dufferin County will agree to speak of in anything more than the vaguest and most cautious of tones. The brief, infamous shot showed Dale Westin — seeming to vibrate and hum at the same low, sacrosanct frequency that had come from the Kersey Ham as he'd borne it up onto the steps of the gazebo — smiling his curious smile, raising one hand to wave at the crowd that was tearing itself apart in front of his eyes, and placing the other, slowly and with something like reverence, on the glazed surface of the ham.

Forensics detectives, holy men called in from Rome, psychics, seers, and Sheriff John Bays Jr. all saw this footage, and were given full access to the gazebo and its grounds in the rueful days after the riots had finally subsided. But although all could plainly see the great glittering leg bone of the ham lying in the dirt, nested among tattered bits of partisan signage, none could find any trace, not a hair nor a thread of high-quality silk, nor a stray molar capped in silver, of the man called Dale Westin.

5.

The events of that spring gave Dufferin County and the town of Bedford a lasting infamy, a pall of the macabre that made visitors driving through on their way to their cottages shiver when passing the town square. A newly launched Ghost Walk, which concluded at the famous gazebo, fast became Bedford's number one tourist attraction. Tabloids hounded Sister Mary Beth Boultbee—who, among everyone, was surely the most deserving of a little peace and dignity—even after she transferred to a parish in Belleville, some three hours east. The newshounds followed her there, and for months she was unable to walk to the laundromat without being photographed, harangued, accused of ignoble intentions, heresy, and witchcraft, and reminded over and over of the ugly depths of mud and blood and meat into which the church she loved had sunk. From the window of his small room in the Headwaters Mental Health Centre, Jeff Stooley watched the reporters who stalked at the gates, begging for access, for a full three seasons after he was admitted.

The *Free Muskrat* chose to ignore the story entirely, deeming it ghastly and best consigned to the compost heap of memory. The week after the riot, with the gazebo still lying in ruins in the middle of the square, its front-page story was about the arrival of strawberry season and what this meant for the practice of effective bear safety.

In general, the Bedford Ham Riots left so many mysteries and loose ends in their wake that events soon became tangled in a morass of confusion, hearsay, and legend, and the reality of the nightmare began to dwindle and fade. The cottagers started arriving in town to buy groceries and supplies, not wanting their precious summers tainted by morbid scandal. The provincial police wanted nothing more than to go back to forgetting that places like Bedford exist at all, save the occasional case of drunken boating or hunting without a licence, and their officers soon disappeared from town, leaving Sheriff John Bays Jr. to assure any who inquired that there was nothing to worry about, he had matters under control, and in the end wasn't it always better if folks just minded their own beeswax, anyhow.

Yet, again, one story lingered among the locals. Although the town was eager to put the past behind it, one big question bit at them like an invisible mosquito hovering around and buzzing in their ears until they'd slap themselves ineffectually, unsure of what they'd heard.

Everyone wondered: what had happened to Dale Westin?

Speculation ran rampant as to the fate of the doomed ex-CEO from the city, who had so briefly but intensely emerged to turn the dials of Bedford's fate as easily as one adjusts the colour on an old television to a garish extreme. Officially, the case remained open, with not a lick of evidence to suggest that he had indeed met his demise among the ham-crazed throngs of the St. Ignatius Annual Easter Picnic Auction. Some believed he had gone back to the city to find solace in the private clubs and office towers from which he'd come. Others claimed he'd taken to the woods to wander like a shaman, existing half in the corporeal world and half in the realm of the spirits, to take stock of the doings of the spruce trees and the squirrels and those lost in the forest, and to win dominion over them.

But the popular opinion among those who'd been at the auction that day was that Dale Westin had somehow fused with the Kersey Ham, his flesh becoming integrated into the sweet honeyed meat, so that the man and his prized specimen, his symbol of country virtue, his tangible and delectable campaign promise, had become a single being some moments before the ham had been ravenously torn to shreds and ingested by those under its spell, and as such that he now literally lived within the people of Dufferin County, like a tapeworm or a deity, guiding their lives and feeding off their goodness and greed, intervening in their love lives and causing runs of good and bad luck, plenty and want. Still others, dismissing the preceding explanation as the product of a collective imagination perverted by too much Hollywood trash, were certain that Dale Westin was still hiding up at his lodge next to the Kersey farm, given over to life as the town recluse—although this theory became less plausible after, on top of a big *FOR SALE* sign going up out front of the padlocked gates, the town election came to pass, yielding its strange and troubling results.

In dealing with outsiders, the residents of Dufferin County had largely taken their cue from the *Muskrat*, forming a silent covenant that forbade open discussion of matters best forgotten. So it was nothing short of flabbergasting to the world at large when, on the night of the municipal elections, by a margin of nearly 65 per cent and with the highly unusual distinction of having garnered all of its votes as a write-in candidate, the winner was none other than—as the voters had unanimously christened it—the Last Ham. This caused chaos among town administrators, who at first saw no way to uphold the results, objecting that the Last Ham was now nothing but a leftover shank bone and a bit of attached femur, hardly fit to occupy public office. Their objections were met with silence from the townspeople: not the hush of consent, but a sharp and furious silence, loaded with the threat of wolves in captivity whose hunger has gone unanswered for too long and who are ready to make a meal of their master. After six town council meetings and much backroom discussion, it was ultimately decided that the result would stand. The incumbent, Mayor McMurrich, was allowed to retain a position as deputy mayor, in charge of acting as a liaison between the ham and the people. The bone from the Last Ham was placed in a glass box in the foyer of City Hall, where all televised press conferences, public meetings, and other matters of government are now conducted.

Last week, a *SOLD* sticker appeared on the sign hanging outside Dale Westin's lodge—identical to the one that appeared, on the very same day, on the matching sign out front of the abandoned Kersey farm (and let it be said that no one begrudges Helen Kersey the money she'll need to rebuild her life in Los Angeles). As for the buyer, the identity hasn't yet been revealed—but there's a rumour that says the two properties have been purchased by the same entity. They say the land will be razed and that an outdoor mall of big-box stores will go in, to service the cottagers who've reached retirement age and want to spend their golden years in the comfort of their winterized retreats. They say it'll bring a new world of convenience and prosperity to Dufferin County, that it will create jobs and lower taxes, that the economy will grow like never before. They say construction will begin in the fall. They say the mayor's office has already approved the deal.

Lehaki Sinking

Atiu crouched by the trickling stream, poking a branch into the water to prod at a huge crab hunkered in the mud. The palm leaves rustled above, scattering glyphs of light across the water's surface, whispering a caution the boy could not yet hear. Saying, *Listen: there is no luck to be found in this stream snaking in from the ocean. No good fortune in the rills cutting so close to your house, closer every day.*

Viliamu leaned in the doorway, watching his son. Atiu's knees were still knobby like a child's, but his shoulders were beginning to grow wide beneath his T-shirt. Next month, he'd turn twelve. Twelve years since the gods had made a barter of Viliamu's life: his wife, Syda, in exchange for a son.

A breath of wind swept scents of plumeria and hibiscus into Viliamu's nostrils, cloaking the musk of mouldy wood and sewage that had permeated the island air for months. He breathed in the flowers' perfume, trying to hold on to it for longer than the breeze allowed. His mind reached for other scents, all rarer now than they should be: taro fried in coconut oil, shrimp fresh from the bay, ahi wrapped in banana leaf and grilled over hot coals. Essences of the island, which Viliamu would always associate with Lehaki, no matter how high the water rose.

He felt guilt in his guts, the same pang that had clawed at him like a burrowing rat ever since he'd gotten the call, two weeks prior, from Baptiste, Syda's cousin who worked as an aide to President Munan. For the hundredth time, Viliamu tried to smother his conscience with resolve. He had no idea what mess he might be making for Atiu to clean up. But he had to try something — that was decided—and though he could see little hope in the plan, it was still better than waiting around for men in tailored suits to come and place death in his son's hands like a rotting fish.

Viliamu's pocket whirred to life. He glanced at his watch. Right on time. He pulled out the old Motorola that Baptiste had given him, shook his head, and snapped the phone open.

"The plane is on schedule," said Baptiste's tinny voice. "Hits the tarmac at noon. Be there half an hour before that. Once you have the Under-Secretary, come straight here. Official reception will be waiting at the front doors."

The line clicked dead. Viliamu sighed. What was there to say, anyway? That no matter what orders the UN gave, he was beholden to the island of his birth, as his father had taught him? That welcoming these diplomats to Lehaki was like laying a red carpet for an armada come to spike the loam with pox-ridden flags? That all of this was an offence to Syda's memory?

He looked once more at Atiu mounding wet sand from the shallow stream bed to form a ring of squat, ever-collapsing castles around the burrowing crab. Viliamu would go to him now and say that the VIP man was waiting. That he would be back late, very late. There was more, much more, but Viliamu had to trust that the palms would speak it for him. They were under siege, too. He whispered a quiet prayer for his son's future before walking over to tell him that there was canned curry for dinner, and to remember to call his Aunt Teata in the next village in case of an emergency.

✕

The palms had been saying much to Viliamu lately. Desperate words. Mad words. They lined the road to the capital, and Viliamu listened to their hissing breath, a fevered susurrus in the breeze. They had spoken to him of a dark shape on the horizon—a bad god, a boar with blood-slick fur and sulphur on its breath, that would come singing a comforting song while sharpening its tusks on the bones of Lehaki's elders. Now, though, the trees' sound was wordless, a low weeping, mourning the arrival of the Under-Secretary, who sat in the back of the scuffed white jeep, clammed up behind his black sunglasses, glowering out the window in silence and flicking sand off his Armani suit. Viliamu had been hired to ferry him incognito to the capital, where they would rendezvous with Baptiste and an entourage of three. It was a covert safety measure, decided on after some of the less subtle islanders spray-painted threats and curses to the UN on the side of the Government Building. Viliamu was the perfect choice. He'd driven dignitaries for Baptiste before, but much of Syda's family saw him as a harmless rube. Jolly but simple, a bit pitiful. They'd never peg him the dangerous type.

The Under-Secretary was from Africa, some drought-ridden, war-torn republic on the South Atlantic. Viliamu had wondered how hard it would be to go through with everything if the man insisted on talking about his own family, or asking after Viliamu's—whether he could carry out the plan, with Atiu's name on his lips. But this dour messenger was easy to dislike, a bored spider wearing navy pinstripes in thirty-five-degree heat, occasionally glancing at the glowing brick of his phone and muttering about the Wi-Fi.

Viliamu checked the rearview mirror to see if the man noticed him taking the exit that led away from the capital, to the island's interior. Nothing. The whole UN, they had no sense of the island's shape on the ground, knew it only from paper maps and prepared speeches. This man had never been to Lehaki before, was here only to proclaim its demise.

It wasn't until Viliamu turned onto the dirt sidetrack, where the palms were so thick that they smacked the sides of the car in crazed applause, that the Under-Secretary spoke up.

"Is this the quickest way to the capital?" he said, in an accent tinged with British, Dutch. His brow furrowed like a squished pudding.

"I understand there are serious infrastructure issues with the flooding, but I was told that the convoy was direct. My men are waiting, and the president will be eager to receive me." He scratched the side of his chin with a long, cola-coloured ring finger.

Viliamu smiled and kept driving, as the car bounced over churned-up mud pits and fallen branches.

"Don't worry!" he said, thickening his accent. "Almost there. We on island time!" He laughed and drove onward into the bush, projecting the dumb confidence that was expected of him. It seemed to calm the Under-Secretary, who sat back and settled into hammering at his phone. Always the damn phone, thought Viliamu. As though the whole world were in there, instead of all around them, in the sea air and the frigate birds soaring in the blue sky and the warmth of the cursed sun.

The Under-Secretary didn't stir again until Viliamu rolled up in front of the little cinderblock hut, cranked the handbrake, and turned to him with the pistol in his hand, telling him to put his phone down and get out of the car slowly, if he wanted to keep his motherfucking guts inside his belly.

✕

After that there was much talk.

"We understand your position," said the Under-Secretary, much too calmly. "But you must understand ours. My visit is just a formality."

Viliamu sat across from the man, pistol poised, while Kolone finished tying him to the chair. As soon as they'd gotten him inside under the bare bulb and ordered him to take off his blazer and sunglasses, Viliamu started seeing details he couldn't afford to notice. Like how the man had a long, raised scar along his left cheek, and deep eyes that didn't waver, even when Viliamu poked the muzzle of the gun right into his nose. Or how he spoke in a dry, rational tone that said he didn't believe for a second that Viliamu would hurt him.

"I know it is frustrating to you," the man said. "But hostility is not the answer. It is my duty to paint for you as clear a picture as possible, in the interest of moving beyond our impasse."

Kolone tested the knots and came to stand beside Viliamu, brandishing his rusted machete like a shaman's staff. They'd agreed that since Viliamu was in charge of taking the hostage, Kolone would do the cutting, collecting blood in bowls to take out and pour into the streams down the road from their village, which had widened into rivers over the past few months, sending tributaries over the paved roads at the edge of town to seep under doors and lick at people's feet.

"It is sinking," said the Under-Secretary, his eyes trained on Viliamu's. His irises were dark and clear, the whites around them bright and sure as the clouds ferrying past Lehaki toward the huge, solid continents over the horizon. "Our early projections suggested we had a few years to address the problem. But if the latest report is correct, we may be looking at a matter of months."

Viliamu scowled. As if he needed to be told. As if there were no swamped huts abandoned along the shore, no mould crawling up the walls of his house, no drowned taro patches, no salt in the wells. As if he couldn't smell it in the air, the jet fuel and luxury cologne stink of men like this one, enveloping Lehaki, tainting the breeze. As if his stomach didn't curdle whenever he looked over at Atiu playing in the precious, dwindling sand. He clenched his teeth. *Don't think about the boy.*

"We can't simply let you stay here, on an island that will soon be erased from the map," the Under-Secretary said. His brow creased further, his eyes burning with some deep, acrid memory as he stared at the concrete wall, but not — past it, into the invisible distance. He shook his head. "You think you are the only ones," he said. "But your sea is not the worst of it." He looked back at his captors. "In my country, millions are dying from drought. This is bigger than you. We are all affected, all implicated. We all must adapt."

Viliamu tried not to listen. The plan would only work if he stayed focused on the truths he knew. Even if this crime — kidnapping, murder — meant his doom, at least it was a doom he could control. As a child, when there were still many elders who knew the island's gods, Viliamu had witnessed the ancient ceremonies, the ones where blood was spilled. The ritual slicing of an animal's neck, usually a pig, accompanied by the speaking of prayers not recorded in any book but passed down through generations, the knowledge thinning out only among Atiu's generation, after the government had banned the practice of traditional faiths. Viliamu couldn't remember all the words, but he trusted that the fragments he could conjure would suffice.

He looked at Kolone, who stood there in his Detroit Tigers cap and floral shirt, machete in hand. Kolone was a tank. Viliamu saw no tremble in his lip, detected none of the doubt that ate his own guts. You could throw a whale at Kolone and he'd stand firm. Viliamu was thankful for his friend's beefy solidity as the Under-Secretary continued his defence, voice infuriatingly calm.

"We are past the point of no return," he said. "I believe you know this."

The gun wavered in Viliamu's hand, as if it were floating in front of him, blown in by the ocean wind. He strained to hear the promise the hissing palms had made: *If you kill the man, say the words, pour the blood out into the hungry sea, the magic will work. The process will be reversed. The sands will multiply.*

"The ships arrived in Fiji yesterday . . ."

The taro will thrive again. Everyone will forgive you.

"They will be here by the end of the week . . ."

Syda will forgive you.

"I am here to assist in an evacuation that has, technically, already begun."

Atiu will forgive you.

"Stop talking!" Viliamu snapped. He closed his eyes and imagined Kolone running the blade across the man's throat, blood pooling in the bowls, the hut filled with gore and the stink of fresh death. He thought of wading through entrails, wet and dead like his flooded taro patch. Rage welled in his chest. The palms hissed: *Do it now. Blood is blood!* Shaking, he brought the pistol up to shoulder height and aimed it at the Under-Secretary's head.

"Don't—"

CROCK-CROCK!

Viliamu stumbled back from the recoil. Debris crumbled and dust plumed from the wall and he could hear Kolone's muffled shouting through the shockwave of gunfire.

Seconds passed and his hearing came back, tinged with ringing. Kolone stood agape, the machete limp at his side, ballcap askew and dripping sweat, staring at the two jagged craters Viliamu had shot into the concrete, inches to the left of the Under-Secretary's head. The man just sat there, unmoving, a new intensity in his eyes, a brutal knowledge smouldering somewhere below his polished facade. He smiled and it terrified Viliamu, whose wrist rang with pain from the force of the shots.

"You think I am unfamiliar with gunfire? Warrior?"

Viliamu tried to summon his rage again, but it was choked, as though the Under-Secretary held it in his teeth. He was setting up a killing blow. Viliamu saw how he let his head drop just a touch, how his eyes softened again, cleared of the hatred that had seethed through them for a second, the ghost of some former self that qualified him utterly to preside over matters of life and death.

"Back home, in Angola," the Under-Secretary said, as though summoning some radioactive nugget from inside his chest to offer to Viliamu like a dark berry, "I have a son. The only one left, of six children. He's just turned eleven."

The word exploded in Viliamu's mind: *Atiu, Atiu, Atiu.*

"If you have a son, do right by him, as best you can."

Viliamu felt a shuddering beside him. He turned and saw Kolone—stout giant, father of two—sobbing. They'd spent weeks working themselves into a blind fever, convincing themselves this was the only way, that any cure from the outside could only do more harm. Whenever the question of their sons had come up, Kolone had always quietly passed the rum and said this was all for the kids, in the end. Now here was his friend, his face folding in on itself like a stepped-on jelly.

On the floor below the fresh bullet holes, a hairline crack in the wall admitted a little gully of water.

Without a word, Viliamu turned and walked out into the blazing afternoon sunlight. Kolone followed. The two stood in the humid day, drenched in sweat, and stared at the thinned jungle, the wilting palms with fungus crawling up the trunks like skeletal fingers. Near the base of a tree with its rotten pith exposed, a drowned crab bobbed in the ripple of the advancing waves, its shell separating away from its inner meat.

"Brother," said Kolone, slapping his Detroit Tigers cap against his thigh, chucking the machete into the mud. "It was crazy, to do this."

Viliamu looked at his friend. He was remembering an old dress of Syda's, bright red and covered in a pattern of green vines and flowers of blue and gold. How she'd shone in it, belly swollen with the life she'd trade for her own. He thought of the blows fate had dealt to him, but to others, too. How time extended backward and forward in great expanses that saw islands rise from the sea and crumble back into it, saw whole nations driven mad with thirst. He thought how little the island's future meant—except to him, except to all of them on Lehaki, their home that would disappear.

"We're dead, all of us here," he said. "Born dead."

Out past the trees, the ocean sighed.

Viliamu clicked the safety on the pistol, jammed it into his belt and went back into the hut, where the Under-Secretary sat, brow barely misted with sweat. He spoke as soon as Viliamu entered.

"If you let me go now, we can pretend this never happened," he said. "I will tell them we took a wrong turn. That the delay was my fault. No one will know what went on."

Viliamu walked over to untie the knots.

"Thank you," the Under-Secretary said. "You are doing the right thing. You have my gratitude." His bonds loosened, he extended his hand. "My name is Gabriel," he said. "Gabriel Lukambo."

As if Viliamu didn't know his name. As if he hadn't known it all along.

"I am here to help," he said. "You, and your families."

But Viliamu knew: there was no helping, now.

He thought of Atiu, and his knees gave way.

✕

Plumeria and hibiscus. Taro fried in coconut oil, crab and ahi cooking over red coals. Mould, salt, fungus, and moss. All of these were scents that belonged to Lehaki now, scents that awoke in Viliamu's heart memories that made up the shape of the island he knew and could not imagine leaving. Yet the one scent that destroyed him, the one that made the island whole and blew it apart at once, was the one that, from this day, would always be missing: the warm, nutty scent of Atiu's hair. Viliamu breathed it in, his face buried in it, as he hugged his son to him for what was probably the last time, feeling the muscles in Atiu's shoulders and back, the heft of a man, though he shook like a frightened puppy.

Out on the surf, the Zodiacs bobbed and whined, packed with more people than Viliamu could count. The only number that mattered was: *most*. Most everyone he'd ever known. Most everyone on Lehaki. They pulled away in waves, like a raid in reverse, buzzing out to the huge cargo ferries moored offshore, which

Gabriel Lukambo, former child soldier turned Under-Secretary-General of the United Nations, had sent to deliver the people from their condemned island. President Munan strode the length of the swamped beach, praising the evacuation efforts, patting the backs of the weeping as they stumbled into boats to nowhere, telling them that some things were beyond anyone's control. Baptiste followed behind him, a hollowed-out look in his eyes.

They all knew full well that Lehaki wasn't sinking. That the sea was rising up to engulf it, swollen by the chunk of Antarctic shelf that had slouched down into the Southern Ocean eighteen months ago. The water was angry, and Lehaki was only the first sacrifice. All those people in Oahu, London, New York, they thought it would never reach them — that the sea could only rise so far. That their cities of towers and light would be untouched. But Viliamu knew better. The sea would come for everyone, in time. Most would flee for higher ground, evacuate their homes, like in Lehaki.

But not all. Some would stand to bear witness.

Atiu heaved with sobs, grabbing at his father's shirt. Viliamu ran his hand over his son's back, trying to calm his quivering.

"Why, why?" Atiu said, over and over, tears staining his face. Viliamu's stomach squirmed like a speared ray. Now, more than ever, he owed his son the truth. *Because our island is dying and I cannot stop it. Because I could not face you, standing on a foreign place, having lived and allowed our home to be destroyed. Because I am powerless except for the hope that you'll keep our story alive for as long as there's dry land to walk on. Because your mother is dead, and I am dead, but you can still live.* Yet he feared speaking would bring emotion over him like a breaking wave and turn his last chunks of resolve to mud. He couldn't risk it.

It had been arranged for Atiu to travel with his Aunt Teata, relocating to a UN-run camp on the Australian mainland. Viliamu knew it would be hard for Atiu, unbearably hard. But it was still more of a future than remained here. Gabriel Lukambo had been right—whether it was sinking or being swallowed up, Lehaki was already gone.

Viliamu pulled back, clenched his jaw. Risked words.

"No matter where you end up, you are my son," he said. "Mine and your mother's. You were born on Lehaki. Do not forget."

"Why can't you come?" Atiu asked. There was no understanding this. Not for years.

Viliamu shook his head.

"I'm sorry," he said.

×

The grey hulk trailed a column of smoke and moaned like a stuck whale as it made its slow turn to begin the journey back to solid ground. Viliamu wondered how long Atiu would stay up on the crowded deck, leaning on the rail, peering back through tears at the row of faces on shore shrinking to the size of raisins. He wondered if somewhere, out in the world, Syda's ghost was waiting for their son, to place a hand on his shoulder and tell him to let go of the past.

There were only seven of them left, all men. Viliamu, Kolone, and five others with too much pride and despair in their hearts, too much love for Lehaki, to imagine themselves as refugees. They stood in a line just above the foamy tide, watching the ferries turn to ghosts in the waning light.

Viliamu was the first to turn around. He scoured the treeline at the edge of the beach, looking for whatever dry sticks remained. Tonight, they would have a fire to honour the old gods, shuck clams for dinner, sit in a circle around the flames to share bottles of rum, chew betel, and discuss the days ahead. Whether they might build a monument to stand over the waves, marking where Lehaki had been; or whether they were better off spreading the sands thin with shovels and hoes. Whether to round up the last hogs for a memorial feast, or to meditate and starve. Whether to speak the names of the loved ones they had watched being taken away—sons and daughters, wives and mothers—or to keep the names locked inside their hearts, and let the palms be their whispering chorus. Whether to sit and wait for the sea to cover their homes in water, or to walk out into it willingly, until their heads were submerged.

The Streetcar Goes Sideways Down Cherry Street

My grandfather used to tell a story about Cherry Street. I don't remember the details—he died years ago, before I left home—but the grand finale was that the streetcar went sideways down Cherry Street. Whether something rammed into it, or it just hopped off the rails, I'll never know. My mother might, but I won't ask her.

If you're not familiar—and some people just don't come down here—Cherry Street runs south off Lake Shore, where the Don pukes out into the harbour, all the way down to the beach, where it loops back on itself. There are more people here than you'd think. In the summer, anyway. That's when you get the suburban clubbers jacked on vodka Red Bulls, gunning their Mustangs down Polson all the way to the pier to pretend they're living in Cabo, which is a stretch, considering you can see the tips of the slag heaps piled along Ship Channel from the patio of the Cabana Pool Bar.

There's no streetcar along Cherry anymore. It's Mustangs now, and buses, though most days not very often.

If you go up Unwin Avenue from Cherry, along the strip of parkland where the rave kids used to have summer parties in the brush next to the sailing clubs, you get to the Hearn Generating Station. The first time I saw the Hearn, it was like coming on some huge alien insect sitting in the middle of the industrial blight, with its massive grey smokestack, the walls so steeped with chemical grime that they're almost weeping. It was like a god, the Hearn: a hidden monster in this city that likes to think it's so polite, so polished. I loved that building right away, even though I was afraid of it.

I guess you could say it's because of my grandfather that I know these places. His name was Joseph—a shitty, boring, Biblical name that didn't do any justice to his rage. He drank Black Label beer, or

Bavaria, which he bought because they had the highest percentage for the cheapest price. One of those beers was probably the first booze I ever tasted. He could be really funny, my grandfather. The Cherry Street story got to be kind of a joke with my family for a while, and some days, the good ones, he would go along with it, setting up the last bit like a punchline: *and the streetcar went sideways down Cherry Street!* That's probably why it's the part I remember. I guess I need a few of those things — dumb little refrains from the life I had then — to counter all the other stuff that screams at me so loudly now, garbled and howling, like wind off the lake slamming into the metal walls of a shipping container when you're inside.

I guess you could also say I know these places because of my mom. Mostly, though, I know them because they're home.

It was a night in June that the festival came. I'd read about it in *NOW* magazine, which I pick up in the store where I used to go to buy Felix his kibble. *Luminato* — what a name. Like an angel of pure light descending on the city. The idea to have it at the Hearn was hatched by a foreign programmer, Jurgen or Juri or something. More a fancy New York kind of foreigner than the Toronto kind, who live in Regent Park and drive taxis to support their five kids. My first reaction to the festival was, *What the fuck, here come the hipsters into the Port Lands now, like a rash.* But when I saw what was planned for the Hearn — who was playing — it made my spine tingle.

Sunn O))) — a band like a planet. Crushing drone metal so loud that, played through the right headphones, it will actually keep you warm at night from the vibrations running through your muscles. Here were these people invading my turf, coming to claim my grimy alien god for their own, by elevating one of my favourite metal bands to the status of an art object. I had to stand my ground. Be present. But it wasn't just that. Sunn O)))'s shows were legendary. They wore cloaks like druid priests and had walls of amplifiers thirty feet high. To see them in the Hearn — in the belly of the monster? It was irresistible. And it would be easy enough to get in: I knew about all the Hearn's holes and portals, tunnels and cracks. I'd spent enough nights inside, huddled into my sleeping bag next to Felix, breathing in the lead particles and concrete dust.

The night before the show, I slept behind a dune on Cherry Beach, around the corner from the Hearn. Usually, I sleep at the Field of Dreams by Orphan's Green, up where Adelaide meets the Parkway. Someone there is always good for smokes or a bit of weed, or more, if you're looking and have the cash. But I wanted the whole day to scope my best entry into the Hearn. So I risked it at the beach, where people are more liable to fuck with you. Luckily, that night was quiet.

On the morning of the show, the sun rose into grey clouds and there was a kind of cool, invisible fog in the air, which kept people away for most of the morning, save a few joggers. I'd had vodka to drink the night before, half an old bottle I'd found discarded under the Gardiner, so I slept until Felix's nudging and whimpering got me up. We ambled across Cherry and up Unwin, and there it was again—the Hearn, in all its monumental disuse. Except, even from the distance, I could see the banner draped from the seven-hundred-foot-tall smokestack announcing the arrival of *LUMINATO*. A fleet of white trailer trucks filled the parking lot. People scurried like bugs around the huge cave of an entrance. We crossed the building's main drive and kept going up Unwin, past the stack, to where you could find access points, maybe an entrance that wasn't guarded, a flimsy barrier to climb underneath. We cased the whole place, going round back to the patchy gravel above the channel side. I found a few potential spots.

It was around then that I realized I'd have to find somewhere to put Felix. Sneaking in solo was one thing; a big shepherdlike mutt wouldn't go unnoticed, even one as skin-and-bones as Felix. It was a tricky proposition. I could try and find someone to look after him, but it was getting late in the afternoon. I wanted another nap before the show, and whoever I asked would want something in return.

Besides, it was the Port Lands. A forgotten zone. I figured he'd be fine, that he could sleep for a few hours and chew on a stick or two while I watched the show. I found a stand of trees where I could stash him, past the Hearn's driveway but not quite into Tommy Thompson Park. I settled in for a bite of jerky, a smoke or two and some sleep, with Felix's paws and chin perched on my knees.

When I woke up, it was almost dark — past eight o'clock. I scratched Felix's ears, found a couple good branches for him to gnaw on, put down an old Tupperware container full of water from my canteen, and tied him tight around the base of a big maple. I told him to stay put. I thought, again, *No one will come out this way.*

That night was an exception, though. Turning up Unwin after I left Felix was like walking into a parallel dimension. People streamed up the usually empty road, all kinds — lots of bearded guys in plaid shirts, as you'd expect, but also a different kind of art crowd, people in suits and dresses of bright colours. They had shuttles running, big ghost-lit beetles creaking up the pitted road. Spotlights scanned the sky above the Hearn, white limbs reaching out into the blackness. I thought how you could probably see them from almost anywhere in the city — how Luminato had invited all of Toronto to come down for their drone metal art show, where the biggest freak attraction was the building itself, as though it had suddenly just appeared a few weeks ago and hadn't been sitting there, dormant, for twenty years, with rats like me haunting its corridors. The night was cool but humid. The smells of perfume and beer mingled with the usual reek of coal tar and tinny water. I had on my big canvas coat and my Jays cap. Around that time, panhandling with a Jays cap could easily win you an extra ten to twelve bucks a day, especially if you were willing to go far enough along the waterfront that you got close to the stadium and hit up people on their way to a game. I figured the cap might help if I got caught sneaking into the Hearn.

As it turns out, I didn't have to worry. I'd planned to get in through a loose panel on the north side, but when I reached the main drive I realized it would be way simpler than that. A huge crowd was funnelling its way into the building like a crawling worm. At a glance, it was plain that the organizers had underestimated the Hearn and had no idea how to control the crowd. People were pushing through, past guards with little electronic scanners who looked completely bewildered. All I had to do was move with the mass. No one said a word; I slipped through on the current.

The building was familiar to me, but that night it felt hallucinatory, like I'd taken some crazy acid. Everything was lit in purples and blues. Art stations were set up in corners decked in foil and wire, with screens hung at odd angles, showing footage in grainy black and white. The sound in the building was immense, even with no music playing. The murmuring of all the people in the crowd rose up to the rafters and flapped up there like flocks of trapped birds. I waded through it, mute, amazed, as always, at how normal people live their normal lives, with their soft wallets and polished glasses and clean teeth. I followed the crowd to the main hall, where the stage was built in the middle of the sprawling concrete floor, flanked by steel pillars that rose up into the shadowed web of the ceiling. Hands in pockets, I stood and waited, hoping someone might hand me a joint before the show.

Even now, knowing how the night ended, I sometimes remember the power of the music, and think how it was almost worth it. As soon as the first crushing notes came out of the speakers, feedback squeal and deafening bass like a goddamn tanker smashing into a pier, plumes of thick smoke started spewing out from the stage. The sound kept getting louder, the smoke thicker, the purple lights deeper and more intense. I've tried lots of drugs, nearly everything you could name — Oxy, crack, coke, heroin, K, meth, morphine, a litre of cough syrup with another of overproof rum — and it was like that, Sunn O))): that feeling of being taken away by something, of being lifted with soft hands into an unknown space. In the feral rumbling of their guitars, my body went numb. At the height of the show, when there was a guy stalking the stage, wearing a horned mask and a cape made of broken mirror shards, holding aloft a light that shone like a fission rod clenched in his fist, I looked up and watched flakes of old paint and rusted metal rain down on the crowd, shimmering crystals of an exploded past, drifting in the purple light. I would have sworn my feet weren't on the ground, that I was ascending; the sound they were making was so brutal that it was holy. I cried that night. Not like I sometimes do — because of cold or hunger or loneliness — but for how beautiful it all was, this city that hated me, that was both the broken place I lived in and the emerald city that all the lucky people never had to leave. Those tears were the best kind of emptying. I left before the show was over, tenderized, hoping to slip out before the lights came on and the spell wore off, before the crowds got thick and we'd all have to stagger back out into the air in a dirty human sluice. I wanted to maintain the feeling of floating lightness as long as I could, stay immaterial, dissolved by Sunn O)))'s pulverizing tones.

I don't remember the minutes walking up Unwin, with the Hearn looming behind me, the band's noise bleeding out into the night. I like to pretend they were blissful. That I spent them looking up at the sky, feeling the damp mist settle on my face like the fallen skin of a nighttime cloud, Sunn O)))'s vibrations flowing through me like a spirit of primeval mercy. I like to imagine I couldn't help smiling — me, third-generation Cherry Street filth — all the way over the scrub grass and into the trees, until I walked into the thicket and saw what the demons were doing to Felix.

I don't know who they were — who would have the gall to wander off from a damn art party into the bush, to let their sickness loose. I know they weren't my people. Their clothes were clean, black, without the ingrained dust you see on us who sleep outside most nights. Their hair had product in it. They wore polished shoes. They probably passed for respectable taxpayers out there in the daytime city, even though they'd found some reason to leave the show and come out into a dark patch of the Port Lands, where they'd found my dog and decided to see how far up his ass they could push a splintered fence picket, while one of them held him in a chokehold and clamped his muzzle shut with a piece of wire, to keep him from tearing out their throats.

Coming on it, I could see the aura around them. The haze. First, it was money: a sickly yellow-green mist. Then it was hate, the cool poisonous gas of the comfortable. Then I recognized it for what it really was: too much fancy vodka, one too many designer pills. Playing at debasement, a night in the wild. These people, who had no idea what it meant to be outside — to be reduced, to do things you'd have once called unspeakable because if you don't, you'll die freezing in a parking lot — these people were violating Felix for fun. I can still feel how seeing the wire cut into his snout sent a sharp pain curling around my own neck, how seeing them jam the sharp picket up his asshole while his whole body quaked and he spat out little foamy shrieks made my guts knot up and sent a hot wetness like gushing blood into my bowels.

When I was young, my grandfather would tell me, sometimes, about the war. He told me about crawling through mud, being a human beetle, his job to find and defuse mines, or trigger them in trying. He told me about watching friends get their heads blown off by bullets he'd felt pass inches from his ear. He told me about hiding inside gutted-out cows while mortar shells popped into the dirt around him, sending up sprays of flesh and earth and metal. My grandfather drank Black Label, hit his wife, terrified his daughter. When he got to the part about the streetcar going sideways down Cherry Street, we would all laugh.

There was a rock at my feet and I picked it up, took three big steps and drove it hard into the temple of the guy holding the picket. He never even saw me — just slumped to the ground like a bag of dirt, the picket sliding out of Felix as he went. His buddy saw me, though. He dropped Felix's head — my dog falling limp to the ground, shaking, blood pooling around his haunches — and stood back. He couldn't figure it out, for a second. I guess he was trying to work out what it meant to be caught, and who had caught him.

Once he realized, he backed away a few steps. But he didn't run. He looked right at me, staring at my face for what seemed like a long time. I wanted to think he was petrified, afraid to move in case I ran at him with the rock, screaming a warrior cry. I was all shaky myself, though, breathing weird, spittle at the corners of my mouth. Everything in me was screaming, but my voice was too locked in rage and disbelief to work, too aware of the only way this could possibly go. Because here's what was really happening: he was remembering me. Taking note of my face, so he could give an accurate description to the cops. The spell held for seconds — me breathing in grunts, Felix wheezing, and this guy just studying me, almost sneering — until his friend moaned and coughed on the ground, and my muscles sprung, the tension uncoiling in a wide arc as I brought the stone down onto the fallen man's temple again, then swung it around and jammed it into his teeth, one, two, three times, the cracking getting more damp and hollow with each blow, leaving a ragged bloody chasm where his mouth had been. When I looked up again, wet warmth soaking my arm, the other guy was gone, torn off through the bush, probably already pulling out his iPhone to call 911 and tell them a homeless vagrant was trying to murder his friend.

The picket man had gone still on the ground, so I picked up Felix. He was heavy and light at the same time, and he shook like there were wires pumping volts into his pink belly. I ran with him in my arms, sweating in my canvas coat, up Unwin and toward the spit, out past the marina and into Tommy Thompson Park, boots hammering on the gravel like stone clubs, Felix's limp legs jiggling with each step. My chest was burning so bad in the damp air I thought I might have a stroke, but I didn't stop until I got out to the ragged tip of the Leslie Spit, where it's all stone and fern and prickly scrub and garbage, residue of fleeting camps for people like me; birds and muskrats, lake and sky. The moon was up by then, a soft white disc in the black morning that cast a pearl sheen over the skyline. The CN Tower blinked to the west, above the dark mass of Ward's Island.

Right across the outer harbour, also blinking, was the Hearn. I kept looking up at its stack, as I hunted for a soft patch of grass in which to lay Felix down, crouched by the water and cupped handfuls into an old tin mug, poured the water over my dog's bloodied wounds and put a hand on his heaving chest, saying his name over and over and telling him it was going to be okay. I figured he'd live through it, tough old dog that he was. I looked at the Hearn and asked it, grimy alien god, to make my friend okay, to keep him alive. It answered with more blinks, flashing hiccups of white and red. I couldn't tell if they were a message from its insect heart, blips of recognition, or signals of the new plague being born inside it, the consuming energy that would spread out from its illuminated core and erase the port I knew, bringing more festivals, more parties, more rituals of the unhungry world, casting us faded people out even further from the city to make room for monsters in designer glasses, who drink vodka Red Bulls and Bacardi with lime, escape reality when their tickets allow, and rape the odd dog for fun.

They want to make the city all pretty and smooth, these people. They want to pretend everything is under control, that their buildings won't come alive and consume them. That their skin will keep their corruption contained. But I know there will always be wild places, cracks where things get through, spots that get forgotten, where aberrations go to thrive.

Felix died two days later. I wanted to take him to the vet, but I had no money, couldn't collect nearly enough, even with a tear-stained face and a bloody dog dying on my lap. For some reason, watching Felix finally stop breathing was what got me remembering my grandfather's streetcar story again. I keep thinking how, when I was a kid, the story seemed to have happened so far in the past, in a different place, a different world—but how, actually, it's still happening now. How, in my grandfather's city, the streets have all the same names as the ones I know and live on. How the Hearn lived out its whole cycle of use in the time between my grandfather's childhood and mine. How there was a streetcar here, in his day, where there isn't one now.

Some people have tried to tell me there never was a streetcar on Cherry. That my grandfather must have been wrong, or just made it up. I tell them I remember how it went. *The streetcar goes sideways down Cherry Street.*

I keep waiting for it to appear, that streetcar. Thinking that one day soon, I'll be walking along the pier and it'll screech over the Don, going sideways, and barrel down the road, translucent as a ghost, slicing through buildings like projected light, until it gets to me and I feel myself sink into its ghostliness and become inseparable from it. How I'll find my grandfather inside, smiling—and maybe the angel, Luminato, and my dead dog, too.

Across

Agnes

Agnes stood on the tarmac, staring at the mouth of the Rainbow Bridge. Customs gates cut across it like the teeth of a shredder. The car idled beside her, pushing more heat into the already scorching day. In the distance, the falls roared, as always. Across the border, stateside, the fibreglass curve of the Waterdome peeked out from behind the bridge's towers, swollen and blue, a bulbous wave. In the belly of that dome, you could get right up under Niagara Falls—it was the only way, now—but first, you had to get across.

On this side was Clifton Hill, ice cream, peppermint fudge, french fries and ketchup, clowns and balloons and haunted houses. The best view of the real-life roaring water. But no futuristic Waterdome—no *Immersive 360° Journey Under the Falls*—which was all Callum wanted. His fevered request.

And she had to tell him: they couldn't get across.

He was in the back seat, smacking his sweaty calves against the fake leather. Looking out at her, looking at the bridge.

"Mommy?"

She had to tell him.

✕

Callum had gotten the fever four nights ago, shivering under a teal polyester blanket in their cramped, un-air-conditioned apartment at the edge of Welland. She'd brought him into her bed—a habit that'd stuck, with just the two of them, even though he'd be turning eight this year. It was the heat radiating off him that made her slip. There was no knowing worry like that until you'd slept in it, cooking in it, yellow with it. Callum had looked like a child of three again, his eyes wide, his barely muscled chest puffing like the crop of a mute bird. He was so weak, half-delirious, this kid who was all hers—her one blond grace in a life spent courting losers, running into police caravans and ending up alone in a grey cell with only the surveillance cameras to talk to, and alone again after that.

For feverish Callum, her lone angel, burning alive? She would've said anything.

When he'd muttered about the Waterdome—how cool it was, how badly he wanted to see it, his temperature dropping by a few degrees with just a mention—it seemed like a divine solution. Of course, angel. We'll go see the dome. Anything you want.

She hadn't thought for a second about the border. Her record. Barriers laid in the past.

×

She's ready to fly. One kilo strapped to her back under chute and another tucked between her breasts, zipped into her jumpsuit. The Cessna's propellers give off a deafening whine. From up front, Glen, headphones on over a battered Bills cap, throws her a big thumbs-up.

She looks out the hatch and thinks how she's never seen skies so blue. The clouds curl into charging buffaloes of white mist below her. She can feel the power of the engines running through her hips, vibrating in the straps against her shoulders. The jump is no different than hundreds she's done before. It's like a tandem, but with bundles of kush strapped to you instead of a human being. The contact is waiting in the field below. The only risk is on me, she thinks, and steps out of the plane . . .

She drifts down, warm air wafting up under her purple chute, thinking how the cars down there look like insects, tiny black-and-white things in formation. The sirens flare on, wailing shocks of red and blue. A muffled voice erupts from a bullhorn. She's headed straight for the middle of it all. As she falls, she thinks how there can never be enough light in the sky to make you invisible...

When she told him, Callum's wail blended in with the roar of the falls, gave off mist like the plunging water. It was the kind of moment that he would always bear, her confession lodged in his memory like a splinter: the day Callum Davies knew his mother for a liar and a crook.

Afterward, with Callum still howling in the back seat, she'd driven south along the Niagara Parkway, past the falls. On the boardwalk, where the boats had once departed for rides into the mist, a cluster of demonstrators held poster boards and chanted slogans lamenting the swollen river. They were a permanent fixture now. And they were right: the water was rising. Volume had increased. Flow was unpredictable. Shutting down the tour boats wasn't the half of it: four people had been swept away already, three tourists and a sanitation worker. More would surely die. But Agnes didn't know who these people were chanting at. The government? The falls? It roared back; it would consume them all. No wonder the New York tourist board had built the sleek dome theatre to replace the tour boats, and relentlessly advertised it to the kids of the Golden Horseshoe as a marvel of advanced cinematic technology, a safe and novel way to see the wonder of the great cataract. It was immaterial, empty, a pristine projection devoid of the true power of the water; but no one would die from it.

The falls had no answers for Agnes, offered no magic bridge or levitating mist, so she turned around at Kingsbridge Park and looped back to drive onto Lundy's Lane from the west. Callum's protest had ebbed to a soft warble. She pulled into the parking lot of the Flying Saucer diner, hoping some cosmic junk food would help soothe his wounds.

"Feel like some grub, kid?"

That won a pause in his whimpering, even the hint of a smile.

"Is it a spaceship, mom?"

"Close enough. Come on."

She hauled him out of the car and into the Saucer's dining room, where dozens of families sat, drinking sodas and scarfing fries. They all looked so happy. Whole. Agnes felt her chest constrict, her shoulders tense, was suddenly hyper-aware of her leg tattoos and undyed roots. A waitress came up, glanced back at the dining room.

"Got a couple seats at the bar," she said.

Agnes nodded. They were always bar people.

It went fine through the sitting down and looking at menus and ordering Cokes and cheeseburgers, right up to when the TV above them filled with a picture of the sleek blue dome, its exterior alive with projected light. *"Immerse yourself in the wonder of Niagara Falls,"* said a soothing voice. *"A marvel of technology that brings you below the flow. The 360° Waterdome. ONLY in Niagara Falls, New York."* She watched Callum's eyes go dark and his shoulders slump again, lines of frustration cut into his face, mapping disappointments he understood and did not.

Glen had come to visit her just twice in Millhaven. Once right after she'd told him she was pregnant, once three weeks later. Both times, sitting in the plastic visitor's chair in the same dirty Bills cap he'd been wearing during the flight, talking about how excited he was, how amazing it would be. How *of course* he'd be there for the kid. How sorry he was that Agnes had taken the fall for them both. How he'd make it up to her—not by turning himself in, of course. That wasn't possible. Somehow, though.

The water had been rising ever since Agnes jumped out of that plane.

She tried again to explain.

"You know your mom isn't perfect," she said to Callum. The door to the Saucer's kitchen sprang open and the smell of grease wafted out at her, settling thick and oily on her skin. "What I did when I was younger, it was stupid. I didn't know then, that you'd be here. That it would end up on you. I know it's not fair."

"I could go without you," he said.

She considered him. She had no idea where he'd gotten his blond hair—Glen's hair, when he was younger, maybe. Or maybe Callum was just growing into his own creature, in defence against the defects of his parents.

"Not without me, kid," she said. She'd thought about sending him over alone, watching from the border as he crested the curve of the bridge. Waiting the hours for him to come back. She always got to the part where he didn't. The exercise stopped there.

"It's not fair," he said, as though she hadn't just told him the same thing.

The burgers came and she ate them both, Callum sulking behind his milkshake.

✕

Later, when the sun was low over the river and a sheen came into Callum's eyes, she drove them to Clifton Hill. The air was still hot and the tourists were thick and jostling, but the aroma of funnel cakes and the pulse of music pumping out into the avenue and the *ka-ching!* of arcade games gave everything a softness. You could always be young here; the falls would always be older. She wanted to believe that there would always be bells and lights and candy for sale. But you couldn't stay in this kind of place—not with the grey past behind you and the border in front, with the river engorged and the Waterdome looming, a rigged choice between a future worshipping empty light under a fibreglass carapace, or drowning.

When she saw the red door with the sign overtop, the name hit her like warm fuel.

MADAME PSYCHE
Palm Readings Tarot Fortunes Told

All the sounds around her dilated and mixed. Her back muscles shifted, aching for new alignment. She squeezed Callum's hand. He was in a daze, so tired. Inside, he could sit and rest. The falls roared at her. The border leered. The red door, nested in the shadows of a crook between a candy shop and a wax museum, drew her like an open palm. She needed *fortunes told*.

Up the street, an automated barker called: *SEE!! The most a-may-zing...*

"Cal," she said. "Want to sit down for a bit, hon? Mom wants to go in here."

The red door whispered, *Yes.*

The light inside was haunted red, blood in yellow water. Shadows webbed the jewelled chandeliers, the few working bulbs glowing gold halos amid grey, burnt-out cousins. The smell of incense was thick and sweet. The circle of light around the central table, cast by a red glass lamp, was the only tangible universe. Callum sat on a mound of tasselled cushions in the dimness behind them, watching as Madame Psyche stroked his mother's upturned palm, eyes closed. Channelling secrets. Agnes, tired, let herself get lost in the spell. There were answers here; you could buy them for twenty dollars a half hour.

"I sense a burden in you." Madame Psyche's voice was like a pearl cloud, deep and smoky. "You are being...pulled apart somehow."

Agnes nodded.

"You bear fierce love in your heart. But a piece of you is lost in time. I see you in a blue place. A vast blueness. You are light, weightless...in trouble."

Agnes frowned. She heard Callum rustling behind, turned and checked on him, locked eyes: *we're okay.* When she turned around again, a blast filled her ears, a huge mechanical roar that blurred her vision and pressurized her chest. She knew the sound. Glen's Cessna, barrelling south, hauling skunky cargo to the cross-border market. She was inside. Young. On an adventure. Then, six sirens blaring on, one by one. The sound echoed in her head like mad laughter, swirled around to mingle with Callum's injured wailing, with the roar of the falls, with Glen's chopper-blade laugh as he threw her a thumbs-up from the cockpit and then again through the Millhaven visitation room's Lucite barrier: *a-MAY-zing!*

She grabbed the lip of the table and took a deep breath. Madame Psyche gave a curious look. In a sliver of silence, Agnes's eye caught the figure of another child, standing behind the fortune teller in the dark doorway to an interior room. A girl, not much older than Callum, long black hair falling almost to her waist, green eyes gleaming in the lamplight.

Madame Psyche turned and frowned.

"Sofia! You know not to bother me when I'm with clients."

"Sorry, Mama."

The girl paused for a second to look at Callum huddled in the cushions. Then she was gone, ducked back behind the inner door. Agnes looked at Madame Psyche, who was staring quizzically at where her daughter had been.

"My apologies," she said, fingering her hoop earrings. "I'm not sure when to begin teaching her the family business. Or if I should at all." Some of her mysticism fell away, and Agnes saw the plain beauty of a mother puzzling over her child.

"It's okay," Agnes said. "How old is Sofia?"

Madame Psyche smiled. "She'll be nine next month."

"Callum is seven," she said.

"Hi," he said, sleepily, behind her. Always listening.

Agnes looked up at the ceiling. She felt the darkness press on her, the damp weight of Millhaven. Out of habit, she folded her hands in front of her on the table. Inside was Callum, a tiny figurine, cocooned by the skin and bones of her fingers. When he was born, she'd held his warm body for just an hour before they took him away. For the first three years of his life, she'd known him only in the hard fluorescence of the visiting room, a small creature in the laps of her tired, disappointed parents, leaving him over and over again to walk back to her grey cell, escorted by silent guards. She'd gotten out early for good behaviour, and since then she'd held flesh and blood Callum as close and as much as she could. Still, she would always carry a miniature version of him in the hollow of her palms, a weightless sprite containing his essence. That, at least, was a thing prison had taught her: there's always something they can't take, something only you can create.

She felt tears coming.

"What if I die before I can fix it?" she whispered to her folded hands, wetness on her cheeks. "What if I can never get across?"

Madame Psyche sighed. She leaned in and put her hands on Agnes's.

"Look," she said. I don't usually give out this kind of advice. My trade is...inexact. But I talk to a lot of people. I'll tell you what I learned. My guess is, you've made mistakes. We all have. You're no angel. No devil, either. You've made sacrifices, like any mother." She sighed. "People like us, we live with ourselves. But we're changed by what we love." She pressed on Agnes's hands with a strength that Agnes felt resonate up her arms and through her back.

Agnes sat, stunned in a momentary suspension of time. She'd come for answers. There were none to speak of. Nothing resolved. Some things would never be resolved. But hearing this woman talk, honestly, of love—it was as though a great spring was uncoiling inside of her, a release of some torqued constraint that had held her to the ground since the day she jumped. Warmth bloomed along her spine. The chandeliers tinkled, even though the air was still. She looked Madame Psyche in the eye.

"I was in prison when I gave birth to Callum," she said. She closed her eyes. "He doesn't really understand that yet."

"No. It's difficult, to find the right time."

"He wants to go see the dome."

Madame Psyche shook her head, leaned back, and grimaced. "Goddamn dome," she said. "It's a one-trick pony, a bunch of high-tech hocus-pocus. We've lost 30 per cent of our business over here."

Agnes smiled. "Do you mind if I ask your name? Your real name?"

Madame Psyche considered this, then nodded. "Laila," she said. "Laila Zayid."

Agnes stood, unhooked her purse from the chair, pulled out a twenty-dollar bill and handed it to Laila Zayid, who raised an eyebrow.

"I haven't finished reading your palm," she said.

"Thank you, Laila," said Agnes. "Really. But I'm ready to go now. Callum, hon. Let's go."

×

They walked back to the falls, drifting through the mist and the sounds of the protesters chanting, past Skylon Tower and the strip of big hotels, taking the riverfront park trail out to where the tourist area gave way to decommissioned power stations. Callum, asleep on his feet, stumbled along until she was almost dragging him. She picked him up and carried him on her shoulder, feeling a new strength centred there. They reached the old Rankine Station, a prisonlike brick bunker on the edge of the river. It had been dormant for over two decades. But Agnes could feel energy coming from it, some residual charge that lingered like a spirit around its iron gates. She paused at the mouth of the bridge over the intake reservoir and put Callum down on the grass by the boardwalk. It was late now, the far end of dusk. Most people were clustered in the tourist parks, waiting for the projection light shows to start — or across, on the south side, being awed by the marvel of the Waterdome. Out here, there were only a few stragglers on foot, and the passing headlights of cars over the bridge. Beyond the lip of the gorge, the falls roared, casting up sheets of mist.

Agnes looked out at the far bank. She thought back to the summer of three years ago, to her first few weeks out of jail, when she'd taken Callum to a city park. They were running in a wide sunlit valley. White clouds coasted across the blue sky. There were power lines along the edge of the park, but Agnes had let Callum fly his kite anyway, careful to not let him go too high. She looked up, into that remembered sky, the broad glare of its sun. Then she blinked and came back, to Callum now, in the rose Niagara evening. Maybe the idea wasn't to be invisible, after all. Maybe there was still enough light.

She crouched and squeezed Callum's upper arms.

"Callum, hon, I need you to stand up."

He stood, wavering, and she steadied him and brought him to the guardrail at the edge of the water.

"Now, listen to me. I want you to hold on, Callum. Hold on to me. Do you understand?"

He nodded.

"Okay. Hold on."

She knelt and took him and clutched him to her chest, as tight as she could without hurting. He wrapped his arms around her neck. She could smell sweat and sunscreen on him, feel his breath on her shoulder.

"Hold on," she said.

She hugged him tighter. Inside, she felt a noise, rising. At first, she tensed: it was the same sound from Madame Psyche's, Cessna blades roaring in her chest, paralyzing her. But her muscles twitched, she held Callum closer, pressed him to her torso, and she felt something else there—a rustling, a buzzing, a thing coiling up from within her muscles, threading its way through her. Pain flared in her neck. She cried out and squeezed Callum tighter. A wave of motion rolled over her upper back, pressing upward like fingers through soil. When the two barbed tips burst through her skin, sending spurts of blood across her face and Callum's hair, she started to weep. Her body shook. She wept, tears soaking into Callum's collar, as two spindly tendrils sprouted from her shoulders, dripping gouts of red tissue as their feathers unfolded like the petals of a massive white lily. The falls roared and her muscles trilled with the rumbling in the earth and the rising in her body. Deep in her back she felt new roots fusing to her bones. She wept into Callum's neck, and he cried along with her now, giving little shudders. On a gust of misted wind, Agnes pushed upward, taking her and Callum off the ground. They rose slowly, her wings sounding a low, musical drone, the dusk wrapping around them like an embrace. Agnes looked across, to the flickering dome, then down to the river rushing toward the precipice. She told Callum, *hold on, hold on,* as they rose into the air, weeping.

Up high, in the twilight, the border was barely there at all.

Acknowledgements

To Bethany Gibson, Susanne Alexander, Julie Scriver, Alan Sheppard, and everyone at Goose Lane Editions, thanks for giving this book a caring, attentive home. Many people read these stories as they stumbled toward completion; thanks to all my early readers, especially Dave McGinn and Chris Burt, and to the various editors who lifted the stories with their suggestions, especially Pamela Mulloy, John Barton, Shashi Bhat, and Kathryn Mockler. My copy editor, Peter Norman, made this a much better book. Cheers to Andrew F. Sullivan, Andrew Battershill, and Dimitri Nasrallah for sharing advice on publishing. To Jared Bland, Janice Zawerbny, House of Anansi, Anita Chong, Kirby Kim, Alissa York, Michael Helm, and Tonia Addison: thanks for your help and support. Menon Dwarka: may we find the perpetual lunchtime. Thanks to the good people at the Bristol Short Story Prize and the Writers' Trust of Canada, for programs that create great opportunities for writers. Fistbumps to James Heaslip and Fouad Elgindy for the boss photos. Respect and thanks to Carolyn Smart at Queen's University, whose imparted wisdom grows with time. Thanks to my parents for their unwavering love and to all my friends and family for tolerating the whole writer thing. A nod to my grandfather, who shared some of his stories with me. Everything else to Amy and Danica, for whom my love goes beyond words.

To all the writers out there, locked in rooms, searching for the right verb: I acknowledge you.

"How the Grizzly Came to Hang in the Royal Oak Hotel" was first published in *EVENT*. "Neutral Buoyancy" appeared in *Joyland*. "Home Range" was first published in the *Malahat Review*. "Little Flags" appeared in the *Danforth Review*. "The Last Ham" was first published as a digital single by House of Anansi Press. "Sheepasnörus Rex" was published in the *New Quarterly*. "Between the Pickles" was in the *Bristol Short Story Prize Anthology, Vol. 8*. Thanks to all of these publications.

This book received financial support from the Toronto Arts Council and the Ontario Arts Council, for which I am deeply grateful.

J.R. McConvey's stories have been shortlisted for the Journey Prize, the Bristol Short Story Prize, the Matrix Lit Pop Award, and the Thomas Morton Prize. They have also been published in *Joyland*, *EVENT*, the *Dalhousie Review*, and the *New Quarterly*. McConvey's poetry has appeared in *carte blanche*, *filling Station*, and the *Carbon Culture Review*, and he reviews books for the *Globe and Mail*. In 2016 he won the Jack Hodgins Founders' Award for Fiction from the *Malahat Review*.

In addition to fiction, McConvey also works in film. He created the *National Parks Project*, a cross-platform exploration of landscape, which was narrated by Gord Downie and went on to win a Gemini Award. He has also been nominated for a Canadian Screen Award for *Mission Asteroid* and recently produced five virtual reality pieces for *SESQUI*, a Canada 150 project.

Different Beasts is McConvey's first full-length collection. He lives by the lake in the southwest corner of Toronto.